THE ACCIDENTAL SPACESHIP

by Gene Hunt

Handprint Books 🖐 Brooklyn, New York

Published in the United States in 2005 by Handprint Books
413 Sixth Avenue
Brooklyn, New York 11215
www.handprintbooks.com

First Edition
Printed in China
ISBN: 1-59354-119-8
2 4 6 8 10 9 7 5 3 1

For the children
who listened to my stories.

And for Ann Tobias,
who insisted I keep
patching the holes in this one
until I got it right.

—G. H.

Contents

CHAPTER 1

The Computer Did It

As everybody knows, when an unexpected flying object roars in from outer space and lands in your backyard, it belongs to you and nobody else.

So naturally, when a seven-hundred-foot spaceship landed behind the house where the Smith brothers lived, they owned it. Even though they were only thirteen.

The spaceship landed there because, in a far-off part of the universe, an old computer made a mistake. (Such a teeny mistake, it was! Even now, it's hard to believe it could have stirred up such a big hassle.)

The old computer was the property of The Anytime/Anywhere Spaceship Delivery Company. It did the work that the main office people didn't want to be bothered with. The people in the main office mostly sat around and made phone calls and drank coffee, while the old computer stood in a corner and quietly hummed away. Its job was to send spaceships to exactly the right address on the right planet and to make sure they got there at exactly the right time, on exactly the right day.

Spaceships could be delivered to any galaxy, any planet, any date. It didn't matter to the computer. It may have been old, but it was very brainy.

One day, after it had been humming nonstop for hundreds of years, the old computer went *Click.* With that, it quit humming for half a second. Then it started humming again. The coffee drinkers never noticed.

During the half second it wasn't humming, the old computer was thinking. A brainy computer can do a lot of thinking in half a second, even if it is old.

Click is the computer word for *"Oops!"* So the old computer's first thought was, *Did I say 'Oops?' That means I made a mistake! Nah. Impossible.*

The old computer peeked into its memory. "Will you look at that!" it said to itself. "It's a mistake, all right. I wrote a 'two' instead of a 'three.'" The computer spent a nanosecond giving a computer-style shrug and said, "Big deal."

Quickly recalling what happens to computers that make a mistake, the old computer didn't waste a moment worrying but went straight to panic: "When they find out, I'm doomed!" it shrieked to itself. Then it said gloomily, "They'll unplug me! I'm finished!"

The old computer searched for a way out of its trouble. First it looked for an honest way. Then it looked for a sneaky way. In the end, it settled for a way that worked. "Do they really *need* to know?" it asked itself. Starting to feel relieved, it reminded itself, "This spaceship isn't going on a mission to save a planet from destruction. It's going to a *museum!*"

Feeling quite happy, the old computer thought, *So the museum gets its spaceship in 2005 instead of 3005! People get to see it without waiting a thousand years! How wonderful of me! I should get a medal!* And the old computer erased the mistake from its memory and began to hum again.

The Universe breathed a sigh of relief, and everything went back to normal. Except for a small town in Pennsylvania, where a spaceship was about to land, exactly one thousand years ahead of its time.

CHAPTER 2

The Smith Twins of Whipple Crossing, Pennsylvania

Whipple Crossing, Pennsylvania, is just a little too small to appear on any maps. And it will probably stay that way until somebody builds the museum the old computer mentioned. Nobody knows when that will be.

Whipple Crossing was the home of Vernon and Junior Smith, brothers, also twins, age thirteen. Some twins are identical. They look alike, think alike, and act alike. The Smith twins were the opposite. They were as unlike as they could be. Vernon was shaped in a way that made people who met him think of the word *barrel*. It would be a muscular barrel, but you couldn't miss the resemblance. Junior was the opposite. Built like a hardwood telephone pole, he was tall, lean, and rangy.

Vernon had black hair. His dark eyes were usually found behind a scowl. Junior was blond and usually had at least half a smile on his face.

Vernon was good at coming up with instant plans; Junior was good at making sure the plans would work.

Vernon knew everything immediately and was the first to tell you so. Junior often knew more than Vernon but didn't feel the need to prove it.

Vernon was loud and kind of pushy. Junior was quiet and pretty reserved.

Vernon was born without the gene for patience. Junior got double.

Junior liked to hang around with smart people. Vernon didn't even notice when other people were smart, and for a good reason: He was sure he was smarter.

Each twin thought the other was a little loopy, but they managed to get along. Grandpa had taught them that. A thousand times he told them: "You'll have times when the only person in the world you can rely on is your brother. You have to look out for each other."

Grandpa was all the family the twins had. They were babies when their parents died in a car crash. They had lived with Grandpa in his old farmhouse ever since.

Grandpa was a man with three part-time jobs. He was a storekeeper, a farmer, and a fossil hunter. He kept the store open three days a week. On his farming days, he spent more time tinkering with his antique tractor than he did plowing with it.

The job that Grandpa liked best was fossil hunting. Grandpa was a recognized scientific expert. Every so often, he would go off with a scientific expedition to search for the bones of strange creatures that lived millions of years ago.

When the twins were small, they would stay with neighbors while Grandpa went fossil hunting. One day when they were twelve years old, Grandpa told them, "A little adventure is good for you, boys— and here's your chance! You can come along this time!" Grandpa's scientific expedition made its camp in the Rocky Mountains of Canada. The twins helped with the digging and found a fossil tooth as long as a pencil, but thicker and deadlier looking.

"Wouldn't you love to see the baby this tooth came from?" Vernon exclaimed, holding the tooth like a dagger.

"From a distance," Junior replied. "Not close enough to look in its mouth."

When Grandpa and the boys were at home, the twins helped out at the store. Grandpa taught them all about buying and selling and bargaining. They often traded store merchandise for food the local farmers raised, such as sweet corn in season, or old things from somebody's attic. The store was crammed full of antiques, like sleighs and butter churns. There were also shoes and overalls and tractor parts and every other kind of hardware a farmer needs.

A few days after their thirteenth birthday, Grandpa told the twins, "Listen, boys. You help out a lot here at the store, and you're pretty darn good at bargaining. I'd say you can trade with the best of 'em."

The twins wondered what Grandpa was getting at. He surprised them. "This store is going to belong to you some day. How would you like to put your names on it?"

The old store sign was small: SMITH SHOES & HARDWARE & ETC.

Vernon waited till Junior was off making a delivery with Grandpa, then painted a new sign by himself: THE FAMOUS SMITH BROTHERS MINI-DEPARTMENT STORE.

When Junior saw the sign, he blew up. "What's the matter with you? Are you *crazy*? This isn't a department store! And we *sure* aren't famous!"

"Shoes and hardware—that's two departments," Vernon replied. "Sometimes we sell antiques. And we sell food, don't we? That's four departments! Maybe I should take out the 'mini'!"

"Okay, we have departments," Junior conceded. "But *famous*! How could you say *that*?"

"Everybody around here knows us, don't they?"

"That's not *famous*," Junior protested.

Vernon shrugged. "Sure it is. We're famous around here. Relax."

Junior shook his head. Grandpa just laughed. The sign stayed up.

Not long after Vernon painted his new sign, on a morning when the twins were gulping a fast breakfast so they wouldn't miss the school bus, they overheard Grandpa answer the phone. He started calmly enough but got more and more excited, saying, "What? No kidding? Where? No fooling? Terrific! Starting when? I've dreamed of a chance like this, Charlie. How long do they plan to stay?"

At that point, the excitement went out of Grandpa, and he dropped his voice. But the twins could still make out some of what he said. "I wish I could, Charlie, I just wish I could. But you know my situation. . . . If there ever was trouble with these boys, I'd be too far away. It's just too remote. I can't be out of touch that long. . . . Sorry, Charlie. It's a definite No. . . . 'Bye."

After school, the twins saw how quiet Grandpa had become, and they held a private council. That evening after supper, they ganged up on Grandpa.

Vernon started it by saying, "We know what that phone call was about, Grandpa. You can't say no to a chance like that."

"Like what?" Grandpa said.

Junior kicked the ball along by saying, "Don't pretend, Grandpa. Where's this great expedition going, anyway? Why did you turn it down?"

"Antarctica," Grandpa said. "A mountain near the South Pole. No way you can come. I'd be there at least six months. Much too long for you to be out of school. Bad idea. Forget it."

The twins were ready for this and trotted out one argument after another. Was Grandpa forgetting how they cooked and cleaned and did the wash and everything the time he was sick for a month? Didn't he think they could count on the neighbors? Didn't he think they were mature for their age? Didn't he *trust* them? Oh, did the twins ever have reasons why Grandpa should go on his dream expedition without worrying about *them*!

Grandpa was solid as a rock. It was "No," "No," "No," until late the next afternoon. That was when Vernon said, with a perfectly straight face, "You *owe* it to us, Grandpa. You have to admit, being on our own would be the perfect way for us to learn self-reliance and self-discipline and stuff like that. It's really your *duty* to go."

Grandpa burst out laughing at that one. But—

maybe he was beginning to wilt under the pressure—he did say, "Let me think about it. . . ."

That was the turning point.

Two weeks later, Grandpa was on a plane heading south, the store was temporarily closed, and Vernon and Junior Smith were sitting on the porch of the old farmhouse. They were on their own for the next six months.

"I'm glad Grandpa got to go," Vernon said. "But I wish we hadn't pinned ourselves down to all these rules. This is the same as being grounded."

"It's our own fault," Junior said. "It was our idea to make all those promises. We'd have said *anything* to convince him to go."

"I know," said Vernon. "We pushed too hard. 'Grandpa, we'll promise to be in the house every night by ten o'clock.' School's over, it's summer, so why didn't we say *eleven* o'clock? But no, we had to say ten."

Junior chimed in, remembering some of the promises they had volunteered. "Always make the beds in the morning. Why did we say we'd do it in the morning? Never leave dishes in the sink at night. What difference would it have made if we just said we'd always wash the dishes?"

"No parties," Vernon said. "We could have skipped that one. Grandpa wouldn't have noticed."

"This is not going to be a fun summer," Junior said.

"I bet you're wrong," Vernon said. "Something good is coming. I feel it."

"Like what?" asked Junior.

Vernon thought a moment. "How do I know? Maybe an emergency. Grandpa said we had to keep our promises unless there was a real emergency, remember?"

Junior wasn't having any of that. "Are you *wishing* for trouble? No, thanks."

"A good emergency, I mean. Something that stirs up a lot of excitement but doesn't get anybody hurt. And isn't our fault."

"You don't want much, Vernon."

"You never know, Junior. Anything can happen."

CHAPTER 3

Where Do You Want Your Spaceship?

On most mornings, the first thing Vernon saw from his bedroom window was a big hay field between two long, wooded hills. This particular morning was different: a big dark thing outside his window was blocking the view.

Vernon's shout of surprise woke Junior. Dressing quickly, the brothers raced outside to get a better look. The big dark thing behind their house seemed to be made of painted metal. The metal had a lot of dents, and the paint had a lot of scratches.

The big dark thing was higher than the house. It was very, very long. One end was pointy. The other end had a long, narrow tail. If you can picture a beat-up grape popsicle that's twice as long as a football field and has large windows here and there, then you may be able to imagine what the big dark thing looked like.

A sign had once been painted on the side. Most of the lettering was worn off, but the first two words were still clear: THE FAMOUS.

"Where'd it come from?" Vernon said in a whisper.

"How should I know?" Junior answered. "What is it?"

"I bet I know!" Vernon said. "It's a tank from the chemical plant! It must have exploded and landed here! It just missed us!"

"It doesn't look exploded," Junior said. "It looks. . . streamlined."

Vernon was steaming, not listening. "I'll tell you one thing. That chemical plant is going to get its tank out of here in a hurry. That thing could have squashed the house!"

Junior didn't see the big dark thing as a tank. "Know what it looks like?" he asked. "A spaceship."

Vernon shook his head. "A spaceship? Get a grip! Sometimes I wonder about you, Junior."

Junior went on. "What I don't understand is, what's a spaceship doing *here*?"

At that moment, a door opened in the side of the big dark thing. Above the door, a small sign flashed on. It said MAIN ENTRANCE. A stairway slid out from the door and tilted down to the ground. A deliveryman came down the stairs.

He looked like every deliveryman you have ever seen. He wore the usual deliveryman cap and uniform. He was the usual deliveryman size and shape. He had the cherry cheeks of a deliveryman's face. He walked up to the brothers and said, "Hello, boys. Are your parents home?"

"Just us," Vernon said.

"Well, good," the deliveryman said. "Then you can tell me—this is Whipple Crossing, Pennsylvania, right? The old Smith house? On Smith Lane, a quarter mile from Indian Road?"

It may have been the first time in his life that Vernon couldn't talk. Junior didn't want to. The twins just nodded their heads. Yes.

The deliveryman asked, "Is this okay, behind the house? I can put it on the far side of the barn, if you want."

Vernon and Junior were *still* speechless. They just shook their heads. No.

The deliveryman smiled cheerfully, the way deliverymen do. He said, "Did I wake you up landing last night?"

Vernon and Junior *still* couldn't say a word. They shook their heads one more time. No.

"Good, good," the deliveryman said, still smiling cheerfully. "I try to be quiet, but you know how noisy *this* model is." He held out what looked like a notebook made of metal. Pointing to a large green spot near the bottom, he said, "Thumbprint here, please."

Vernon squinted his eyes suspiciously. "What's this?" he said.

"I need your thumbprint," the deliveryman said. "It shows I delivered the spaceship."

"You mean this really *is* a spaceship?" said Junior. "Hear that, Vernon? A spaceship! A real one!" His eyes were the size of silver-dollar pancakes.

"Sure is," the deliveryman said. "Old *Model 83*. A classic." He looked up at the huge ship fondly. "They don't make them like this anymore."

"We didn't order a spaceship," Junior said. "There must be a mistake."

"No mistake," the deliveryman said. "If this is the Smith house on Smith Lane, this is where she goes." He held out the notebook. "Thumbprint on the green spot, if you please."

"What are we supposed to do with it?" Junior asked.

"With the spaceship? Put it on display, I guess," the deliveryman replied. "Isn't that what a museum does?"

"I don't know about any museum, but I know we're not paying for this," Vernon said.

"You don't pay a thing," said the deliveryman. He pointed to some printing on the metal notebook. "See, right here, they're all checked off. Star tax paid, takeoff fee, license plate, delivery charge, the fuel in the tank, everything—all paid. Pretty nice for a museum, getting a famous spaceship for nothing. Just put your thumb here."

"What's this about a museum?" Junior asked.

The deliveryman looked around. "I guess they haven't built it yet. Don't worry, they will. Look, it says so right here." He held the notebook out for the twins to read. "See? Pennsylvania Classic Spaceship Museum, Whipple Crossing, Pennsylvania. Press your thumb on the green spot."

"I don't know about this," Junior said.

Vernon knew. "Hey, why not?" he said, and pressed his thumb on the green spot. The spot clicked and turned red.

Junior asked, "Who sent this thing?"

"I don't know anything about that," the deliveryman said. "That's another department. I just deliver." He pressed the top of the metal notebook. It hummed, and a silvery sheet slid out. The deliveryman handed it to Vernon. "Here's your copy."

The sheet was as light as paper, but it felt like metal in Vernon's hand.

Smiling cheerily, the deliveryman turned away and walked briskly toward the far end of the spaceship, talking over his shoulder as he went. "Well, I have to be on my way. Good luck with your spaceship. Nice chatting with you."

Vernon looked at the metal paper the deliveryman had given him, and began to read out loud: "'Deliver by noon on July 2, 2005'—well, it got here early, it's only nine o'clock—'Pennsylvannia Classic Spaceship Museum. . . .' I don't know where they got that, but. . . . Oh! Listen to this, Junior! 'Valuable shipment. This is the original Space Brothers ship flown by—'." His voice broke with excitement. "'J. and V. Smith'!"

He looked up with a big grin. "Hear that, Junior? J. and V.! That's us! This is our own spaceship! Is that great, or what?"

To Junior, the whole thing looked like trouble. "Hey, Mister!" he called after the deliveryman. "Hold on! This can't be right! We can't fly a spaceship!"

The deliveryman was just stepping out of sight at the far end of the spaceship. Junior ran after him, shouting, "Wait a minute, will you? I need to talk to you!"

Vernon ran after him, shouting, "You wait a minute, Junior! Let him go!"

Their voices were blotted out by a sound like a giant ripping a stack of telephone books in half. The air shook. After a second or two, the sound faded away. The brothers ran around the end of the spaceship. They saw a round patch, about the size of a wagon wheel, where the hay was squashed flat. They saw a puff of green smoke drifting upward. There was a smell like peanut butter mixed with apples and firecrackers.

The deliveryman was gone. They never saw him again.

CHAPTER 4

The Incredible Language Machine

Of all the odd things the twins found while exploring the spaceship, the oddest was the contraption in a corner of the ship's biggest room.

The contraption was huge. It looked like an overgrown beach umbrella, fuzzed over with a messy tangle of electric wires. The sunshade part seemed to be made of rough green glass. Halfway up the handle of the umbrella was a short crossbar. At each end was an eyepiece—well, it *looked* like an eyepiece, the kind you find on a telescope. Below the crossbar, there was a small red button. Painted on the umbrella platform were two pairs of green footprints.

"What do you suppose it is?" Junior wondered.

"Beats me," Vernon replied. He hopped onto the platform.

"Hey! Don't fool around!" Junior exclaimed.

"Quit worrying," said Vernon. "What, are you scared of an umbrella?"

"That's no umbrella," said Junior. "Better not touch it."

"I'm not touching anything," Vernon said. He stepped onto one of the painted footprints, and exclaimed, "Hey, these are just my size!"

"What are you doing?" said Junior, stepping onto the platform. "What's just your size?"

"The footprints," said Vernon. "Put your feet on that pair and see if they fit you."

"We'd better leave this thing be," Junior said. He put his shoes onto the second pair of footprints. They were the same size as his shoes.

"I'm not doing anything," Vernon said, "just looking." One eyepiece was right in front of him, and he peered into it. "Take a look. This is weird."

Junior tried to look through his eyepiece without touching it. "I can't see anything," he said. To steady himself, he gripped the handle of the umbrella, accidentally touching the small red button.

There was a sudden *whirrrrrr*. The eyepieces beamed a powerful light—light of a color never seen before—into the boys' eyes. The twins could feel something reach deep into their brains. For a minute—it may have been two—they couldn't move. Then the light faded and the strange feelings disappeared. The brothers jumped off the platform.

"Let's get out of here!" Junior said.

"I'm with you," Vernon said.

Later that day, the twins discovered that the green umbrella had done something powerful— to *them*.

The discovery came by chance. An Italian family touring Pennsylvania on vacation made a wrong turn, drove up Smith Lane, and saw the spaceship behind the house. The children in the backseat spotted the huge ship and screamed, "Deesneyland! Deesneyland!" The car stopped.

The father walked up to the porch steps where the brothers were sitting and looked into a little Italian-English dictionary. With a heavy accent, he said, "Hello. . . . You make . . . movie. . . ? Science fiction. . . ? My children see. . . ? Permission? Yes? Please? How much?"

Vernon answered quickly, "Sure, three dollars apiece."

Just as quickly, Junior added, "Children free." That annoyed Vernon, but Junior thought it was only fair.

The brothers watched as the Italian family climbed the stairs to the main entrance. They heard the Italian girl say, *"Mama, lui me spingere! Fanno fermato!"* (Which means something like, "Mom, he's pushing me! Make him stop!") To their amazement, the boys understood perfectly.

The Italian mom said, "*Giuseppe! Lasci il tu sorella!*" (Meaning, "Joseph! Quit pestering your sister!") The boys knew exactly what her words meant.

The Italian boy said, "*So fare niente! Lei iniziare.*" ("I never touched her! Besides, she started it.") Vernon and Junior understood as well as if the words were English.

The Italian dad said, "*Fermateve! Il pagamentosiamoqui per il monumento! Attenzione!*" ("Cut it out! I paid good money for this! Now settle down!") The message was unmistakably clear to the twins.

Both brothers felt a little dizzy. They closed their eyes, gripped the stair rail, and stood still.

The Italian dad saw them standing with their eyes shut and said, "*Puo chiamarmi un medico?*" (Which means, "Are you all right? Do you need a doctor?")

The brothers understood. Vernon said, "*Me sento bene. Pensa un poco.*" (Which means, "Oh, I'm fine. I was just thinking.")

Junior said, "*Grazie. Divertiris le vacanze?*" (Meaning, "But thanks for asking. Are you enjoying your visit?")

The Italian dad smiled and said, "*Si, si!*" (His way of saying, "We sure are!") Then he walked ahead to catch up to his family.

CHAPTER 5

A Spaceship Can Be Boring

A little of the language game was enough for Vernon. He craved action. He spent hours in the spaceship control room, punching every button, turning every knob, twisting every handle. The spaceship ignored him.

"What good is knowing a language if you can't go where they speak it?" he demanded. "You know what this spaceship is? Boring."

Junior started to count the equipment in the control room. "Twenty-seven television screens—I guess they're television screens. That big one has to be fifteen feet high. . . . Forty knobs on the big desk. . . . Twenty-five of these funny handles . . .

forty rows of buttons . . . hundreds of dials. . . . Then there's the robot—"

Vernon looked at the thing his brother had called a robot. "Robot?" he said with a sneer. "Are you serious?"

"If it's not a robot, why does it have a computer screen? And what about the antennas?" his brother asked.

The robot—or whatever it was—stood about as tall as a professional basketball player. It was shaped like a huge tin can, balanced on three smaller tin cans—which stood on what looked like a set of metal Frisbees. The screen Junior mentioned was in the middle of the big tin can. On the sides were two things that might have been snaky arms. At the top was a round bump shaped like an upside-down mixing bowl. The entire robot had the shiny look of a brightly colored tin can.

"Don't be silly, Junior," Vernon said. "That isn't a computer screen. It's a picture frame, maybe. Besides, robots do things. All this does is stand still and look stupid. Look at it! Maybe it's a statue or something. Anyway, it's no robot."

Junior shrugged. "It looks like a robot to me. Anyway, I think all this is pretty interesting."

"Interesting, baloney," Vernon replied. "If we could read these stupid books, maybe we could figure out how to turn this stuff on." He pulled a red book from a pile in the corner and opened it.

The pages were covered with squiggles, like worm tracks. He threw the book back on the pile. "The only thing that works in the whole ship is the stupid language machine!"

Junior sat straight up. His eyes grew wide. "I wonder," he murmured to himself. He picked up a book with a striped cover and walked out of the control room. "Be right back," he said.

Grouchily, Vernon sank down in the most comfortable chair and closed his eyes. He was asleep a few minutes later. He didn't see the green light of the language machine shining beneath the door. He didn't hear Junior shouting, "*Yeow!*"

Vernon only woke up when Junior walked back into the control room staring into the striped book. "What's up?" he asked.

Junior didn't say a word but walked up to the main control board. He found a row of green buttons and pushed the thirteenth button twice. He looked at the striped book again and turned a dark blue knob one full turn. He looked at the book once more, took a deep breath, and twisted a yellow handle to the left.

All the buttons and dials on the control board lit up.

"What did you do?" Vernon shouted.

"I learned to read the book," Junior replied. "I used the language machine. I couldn't believe how easy it was. Hold the book to your head, look in the eyepiece, and push the red button. Nothing to it."

"What does that say?" Vernon said, pointing at the squiggles on the page.

Junior started to read out loud. "'Chapter One, How to Start Your Spaceship. . . . Step One.' Wait a minute." He closed his eyes. "Hey, I don't need the book! I can see the words in my mind!"

"Okay, okay!" Vernon snapped. "Any way you want—read what it says!"

Junior closed his eyes again. "'If you come from a planet where people can tell where everything is by just thinking, skip this and go to Step Two.' How about that, Vernon? They see by thinking!"

"So what?" Vernon asked. "I see *without* thinking! Read the rest!"

Junior began again. "'If you come from a planet where people see by using their eyes'—Hey, that's us, Vernon!"

"Read the book! Read the book!"

"I told you, I don't *need* the book." Junior closed his eyes and continued. "Let's see. . . here we are, paragraph three. 'If you come from a planet where people see by using their eyes, instruct the central thinking unit to turn on the lights.'"

"Central thinking unit, huh? That must be the computer," Vernon said. "Well, start it up!"

Junior thought a few seconds with his eyes closed, then pushed three buttons and turned a knob.

"Nothing happened," Vernon said.

"I just turned on the voice and sound," Junior said. "Now it can hear us, and we can hear it."

"Let's see if it works," Vernon said. He sat back and pointed at the massive control panel. "Hey, computer! Or whatever you are! Say something!"

The tall tin-can thing glided noiselessly to a point behind Vernon's chair. The computer screen in its middle glowed. From somewhere inside, a metallic voice said, "Were you speaking to me?"

CHAPTER 6

I Do the Thinking around Here

Vernon jumped a foot. "Hey! What's the idea of sneaking up on me like that? You think that's funny?" He stared at the tall robot. "I don't believe it. The tin man is the *computer*?"

The robot spoke coldly: "Never call me a computer. Science abandoned mere computers hundreds of years before I began my peerless existence. I am a Post-Electronic Thinking System. I do the important thinking around here. You may call me Thinker."

Junior was instantly excited. "Wow! I'm real glad to meet you, Thinker!" he exclaimed. "My name is Junior. It's a real honor to meet a thinking system!"

"As it should be," Thinker said loftily. "It is good

to meet a person who can appreciate that. Meeting you is a positive experience, Junior."

Vernon broke in. "We don't need a machine to think for us! We can do our own thinking!"

"Oh?" Thinker was scornful. "You can perform the mathematical calculations that space flight calls for, including three kinds of math that no warm-blooded being has ever understood? You are a master of scientific logic? Ha! You can't possibly meet the demands of spaceship thinking."

Vernon never did know how to back down in an argument. "We can think just fine," he said.

Thinker wasn't finished. "How about the essential data that space travel requires? To help you understand the question, I shall explain what I mean by data. . . . "

Vernon interrupted. "I know what data is!"

"Oh?" Thinker's voice was icy. "Then from this location—what's it called? Earth? Silly name—what is the distance from Earth to Galaxy 8995J?"

"How should I know?" Vernon replied indignantly.

"The answer," said Thinker, "is three million, six hundred and twenty-two point four light-years. That is *real* data, and I keep vast amounts of it handy at all times."

"Fantastic, Thinker!" Junior exclaimed. "It must be wonderful to know so much! Can you tell us how come we got this spaceship?"

Vernon didn't like any of this. "Hey, hold it, Junior. We don't need this chitchat!"

Thinker ignored him and turned to the other twin. "I regret to say, Junior, that I am programmed not to answer your question."

Vernon was indignant. "Wait a minute, tin man! Are you saying you won't tell?"

Thinker asked Junior in an icy voice, "Who is this person?"

"This is my twin brother, Vernon."

"Meeting him is a negative experience," Thinker murmured.

The robot pivoted so his screen faced Vernon. "Try to understand, Vernon person. I follow instructions from the spaceship owners, unless my calculations show they would cause the ship to crash or explode. I do the vast amounts of thinking required to keep all systems running perfectly. But even I have a limit. I may not reveal the secrets of people who have been part of the history of the ship. So, yes, I am saying that I won't tell."

"This thing is going to be a lot of help, I can see that!" Vernon exclaimed.

"Take it easy, Vernon," his brother said. "I'll bet Thinker can do a million things."

"It can't answer a simple question!" said Vernon. "Let's see if it can do something besides talk. Okay, Thinker, pay attention. We're the owners; you're the robot. Turn on the lights! And the air-conditioning! And while you're at it, get me a snack! Lights, air-conditioning, snack. Think you can handle that?"

The spaceship came alive. The lights went on. The air-conditioning started to hum. A little door in the back of the control room opened, and a bag of something like potato chips popped out.

"All right!" Vernon exclaimed. "I guess the robot is going to be useful after all . . . no matter how stupid it looks."

"I always try to help those with much slower minds," said Thinker, in a silky voice.

"How smart will you be if I pull your plug?" Vernon retorted.

Junior stepped up to the main keyboard and pressed two keys. The robot froze, and its screen went dark.

"What did you do that for?" Vernon demanded. "This was just getting good!"

"Listen, Vernon," Junior said in a whisper. "You can't get into fights with Thinker. He's important on this ship. Like it or not, we need him. You can't act as if he's the enemy! Understand?"

"Okay, okay," Vernon said.

"Promise?" said Junior.

"Okay, I promise," said Vernon. "No more fights with the computer." He thought a few seconds. "But that doesn't mean I can't argue."

"Okay, you can argue," said Junior. "But no more now. Forget the robot. We have to find out what's in these books."

CHAPTER 7

Real Spacemen Aren't Called Vernon and Junior

Grumbling, Vernon started collecting books. Junior held a button down as he whispered to Thinker, "Don't mind my brother. He's okay when you get used to him. I'm looking forward to learning a lot from you."

Thinker was silent but flashed a little green light as if to say, "That's more like it."

Junior reached for a thin blue book at the top of the stack Vernon had piled up. "This is called *How to Land Your Spaceship without Squashing Anything.*"

Vernon snatched the blue book from Junior's hands.

Junior read the cover of a thin black book. "*If*

You Can Steer a Horse, You Can Steer a Spaceship."

Vernon snatched the black book. "Is there one that shows how to take off?"

Junior picked up the thickest book in the pile. "I'll try this one. It's called *How to Navigate from Star to Star without Running into Planets.*" He took another book, this one only medium-thick. "I think I'll read this first. I like the title, *Eee-Zee Space Navigation for Beginners.*"

"I don't want to be a navigator," Vernon said. "I'd rather drive." He was struck by a new thought. "Hey, this is terrific," he said. "You like navigating; I like driving. We're the perfect team! You can see that, can't you?"

Junior had a feeling that his brother had something in mind besides teamwork. "Maybe," he said cautiously.

"We need better names," Vernon said.

Junior was flabbergasted. "You mean you want to change your name from *Smith*?"

Vernon laughed lightly. "No, no! Never! We'll always be Smith. I just mean—if the name you use is Navigator, people will think you're a navigator kind of person. Right? And if the name I use is Pilot, people will know I'm the driver. Nothing wrong with that, is there?"

"I guess not," Junior said warily.

Vernon went on without a pause. "And, of course,

we need a name for the ship—right, Navigator?"

"Okay, here it comes," Junior replied. "What name do you want for the ship?"

Vernon's voice was so sincere it made his brother uneasy. "I just want to use what it said on that sheet the deliveryman gave us. Remember? It said the Space Brothers!"

Junior felt relieved; he had expected something worse. "The *Space Brothers*? That isn't bad."

"Maybe the *Famous Space Brothers*," Vernon suggested.

"We talked about this before," Junior said. "We're not famous. Outside of Whipple Crossing, nobody knows us at all."

"'Famous' is already painted on the ship, Navigator," Vernon pointed out reasonably. "Anyway, we can't miss being famous."

"Oh, come on!" said Junior. "Who says?"

"That same sheet, that's who. It says the ship is valuable because it was flown by J. and V. Smith! Would they write that if we weren't going to be famous?"

"I don't know what they'd write," Junior said. "Neither do you, Vernon. They delivered the ship to a museum that doesn't even exist. They could get a name wrong."

Pilot wrapped his arms around his books and started toward the language machine. "We'll talk about it later," he said, over his shoulder. "Quit worrying, Navigator! Think big!"

He stopped and looked back. "And let's get in practice, okay? From now on, I call you Navigator! And you call me Pilot!"

CHAPTER 8

All about Hay

The brothers soon found that it took two minutes to learn an entire book on the language machine—thick books a little longer. But thick or thin, every word, every picture was printed in their brains.

When they had finished their books, Pilot was ecstatic. "This is great! We're ready to go! Pack up! Prepare for takeoff!"

"Wait a minute, Vern—I mean, Pilot," Navigator said. "We don't know what the engine runs on."

Pilot peered at the fuel gauge. HALF FULL. "See if you can find a book on fuel," he suggested. "You're better at finding stuff than I am."

Navigator shook his head, sighed, and started searching.

Actually, Pilot was right. His brother *was* a better finder. Twenty minutes later—while Pilot was practicing the moves for reverse-loop turns at 300,000 miles an hour, in spite of Thinker looking over his shoulder in an annoying way—Navigator found the fuel book. It was behind a cookie box in the spaceship kitchen. It was called *Run Your Spaceship on Free Fuel*. Navigator learned it quickly on the language machine.

"This is amazing," he told Pilot. "Know how many places spaceships can get their regular fuel free? Nineteen!"

Pilot smiled. "Free gas! How about that!"

"These fuels aren't gas. They're all different. Powdered rock from one planet, ice from a special comet, things like that."

"But free, huh? Great. How far away is all this good stuff?"

Navigator walked over to the robot. "Can you help us on that, Thinker?"

In a bored tone, Thinker said, "Of course. The nearest source of regular free fuel is three billion, one hundred and seventy-nine million, six hundred and forty-eight miles."

"Thank you, Thinker," Navigator said. "That was so clever! Working it out so fast, I mean."

"Always glad to help out, Navigator," Thinker said, then switched to a whisper, "As long as it's you and not Pilot."

"Hey! Is this a spaceship or a tea party? Did he say three *billion* miles?" Pilot asked impatiently.

"I am not a he. Or a she. I am an it," said Thinker loftily.

"I don't care if you're a zit," Pilot said. "Let's have that answer again."

Thinker replied in a sulky tone. "Distance to the nearest source of regular free fuel is three billion, one hundred and seventy-nine million, nine hundred and ninety-three miles."

Pilot objected, "That's not the same number!"

"While you were having your little tantrum, the planet moved three hundred and forty-five miles away," Thinker replied in an icy tone.

"That does it!" Pilot shouted. "We can't get fuel, and this one has an attitude! Let me tell *you*, metal brain—"

Navigator broke in. "Hold on, brother! I haven't told you what the last chapter says."

"What about it?" Pilot said with a snap.

"The title is *Rare and Unusual Fuels*," Navigator said with a cheerful smile.

"Rare and unusual," Pilot grouched. "A lot of good that'll do us."

"Please go on, Navigator," Thinker said.

"Here's the good part." In his mind Navigator read from the book: "'Although most planets have pink oceans and red plants—'"

"Sounds sick," Pilot muttered.

"Brighter minds find those colors quite beautiful," Thinker murmured.

Navigator continued, "'. . . nevertheless, there is a rare type of planet with blue skies and oceans, and green plants.'"

"What do you mean, 'rare'? Those colors are all over the world!" Pilot interrupted.

"Among the billions of planets in the universe, that color scheme is most unusual," said Thinker.

Navigator started again. "'The early space explorer Parco Molo was the first to visit a blue-green planet. He watched while the natives cut thin green plants, tied them into bundles, and put them in a building where cows and horses lived.'"

"That sounds like hay!" said Pilot.

"And a barn!" said Thinker.

It was the first time they had ever agreed on anything.

Navigator went on. "'Molo took two bundles of green plants back to his ship to study them. As he was walking past the engine, a bundle accidentally fell in the fuel box. It turned out to be the most powerful fuel Molo ever found.'"

"What a wild story!" Pilot said, laughing.

"Hardly scientific," Thinker said. "'Wild' is probably accurate." It was the second time they agreed.

Navigator read on. "'Unfortunately, Molo's notes on the location of the planet were lost.'"

Pilot hooted. "Way to go, Molo! Tell a big one, then lose your notes!"

"A perfect cover-up," Thinker agreed. Third agreement in a row!

"You're probably right," Navigator said. "I'm going to try it." He left the spaceship and headed toward the barn.

When he returned, he was dragging a bale of hay. He heaved it into the fuel box and started the engine. "Will you listen to that!" he said. The engine idled with a deep sound of limitless power. The fuel gauge showed FULL.

Pilot and Thinker were almost too amazed to talk, but they managed a few words.

Pilot said, "When you think about it, cows get energy from hay, why not a spaceship?"

Thinker said, "I believe I see how hay might work. I'd explain it, but I'm afraid you wouldn't understand the math."

That may have been the last time Pilot and Thinker agreed on anything.

Navigator didn't say a word. He just turned off the engine and started dragging bales of hay from the barn to the spaceship. Pilot followed him. For the next few hours, Pilot and Thinker avoided embarrassment by being careful not to look at each other.

CHAPTER 9

Fish Today, Worry Tomorrow

The brothers were now ready for their first test flight. They just weren't sure where to go.

"Cleveland isn't far," Navigator said. "And we already speak the language."

"We can get to Cleveland on a bus," Pilot said scornfully. "We ought to go at least as far as China. Or the moon!"

"The moon is hundreds of thousands of miles away," Navigator said. "You might as well talk about going to another planet."

"Sure! Learn to speak Martian. Why not?" Pilot asked.

"I don't know if we're ready for that," Navigator

said. "Anyway, things might cost too much on some other planet."

"Hay is cheap," Pilot said.

"Sure, but it's all the other things. Like food—what if a sandwich was a thousand dollars? We'd starve," Navigator explained.

"We could get jobs," Pilot said.

"Doing what?" Navigator asked.

His twin had the answer ready. "We could work in a store. We've done that."

"On other planets, we'd be aliens," Navigator said. "They might think we looked horrible. Would you want a horrible-looking alien working in your store?"

"Might be a big attraction," Pilot said. "But I see what you mean. Let me think. . . . "

He sat in his pilot's chair, squinted his eyes, and went still as a rock.

Navigator knew it was no use talking to his brother when he got that look on his face, so he waited.

Ten minutes later, Pilot opened his eyes wide, stood up, and said, "Ha! That's it! It works out perfectly!"

"What now?" Navigator asked.

"It's the perfect plan!" Pilot almost shouted.

Navigator stood up, walked over to his brother, and looked in his eyes. In a soft but very serious voice, he said, "If you don't tell me your idea, I'm going back to calling you Vernon."

"Okay, okay," Pilot said. "Space traders. Isn't that great? Space traders."

Navigator had a sick feeling that his brother had lost a large part of his mind. "What are you talking about?"

Pilot rushed on. "Like the old pioneer traders! They set up a trading post at an Indian village and traded for furs. Then they moved to another Indian village and traded for whatever they had–silver, maybe. Or food. They kept on trading from village to village. See?"

Navigator could hardly believe his ears. "You want to take the spaceship to Indian villages?"

"No!" Pilot shouted. "I want to go trading from planet to planet! We buy, we sell, we barter. Just like we did at the store! *Now* do you see?"

Navigator spoke slowly and uncertainly. "Space traders, huh? Space . . . traders. Uh–what's that *mean*? How do you do that?"

"Simple," Pilot replied smugly. "We buy stuff on one planet and sell it on the next. Then we buy more stuff there and sell it on the next planet."

Navigator knew his brother's idea was insane, but he couldn't resist asking. "How would we get started? What would we sell on the *first* planet?"

"That's part of the plan," Pilot explained. "We

take the stuff in the store along with us! All the shoes, all the hardware, all the food that won't spoil, all the mixed-up stuff in the middle of the store! Everything!"

Navigator was horrified. "Are you crazy?" he said with a gasp. "That all belongs to Grandpa!"

Pilot spoke smoothly. "Yes, and we have to make sure it's all safe, don't we? Well, if we take everything with us, nobody can steal it from the store, right? Besides, by the time Grandpa gets back, we'll have done enough trading to fill the store up a dozen times!"

Navigator was stunned. "Are you serious about this?" he asked.

Pilot counted on his fingers as he spoke. "One, we'd be able to speak the language. Two, we're good at trading. Didn't Grandpa say so? Three, we could travel cheap. There's plenty of room in the ship for us to live."

Navigator looked around the spaceship. "That part is right, anyway. You could fit twenty houses in here."

"Well, that's it!" Pilot exclaimed happily. "That's our plan! We'll be traveling space traders!"

"What if people on other planets don't want hardware or shoes?" Navigator objected weakly.

"That's the beauty of it," Pilot said. "*Everybody* will want something from another planet! Even if it's just for a souvenir! You can see that, can't you?"

"I don't know," Navigator said. "I never heard of space traders."

"Of course not!" Pilot said. "That may be the best part! We could be getting in on the ground floor! Maybe we'll be pioneer space traders! That's how you get to be famous, you know—be a pioneer!" Pilot thought for a moment, then rolled on. "And that means, we need a pioneer kind of name for the ship. We'll call it . . . The Trading Post. No! The *Original* Trading Post!"

Navigator was relieved to find one thing he could agree with. "How about the Space Brothers Original Trading Post?"

"It's perfect!" Pilot cried. "Well—almost perfect. There's only one word that could make it more perfect. You know, Nav, we're going to be famous."

Navigator started shaking his head, but Pilot wasn't going to stop for anything. "Don't say no to fame, brother," he said solemnly. He looked into the distance. His expression made Navigator think of the way Columbus must have looked the day he sighted land. "Think of it. *The Famous Space Brothers Original Trading Post.*"

Navigator kept shaking his head.

"I know, I know," Pilot said. "We're not famous *yet*. You said that before. Look. The word's already painted on the hull. If we don't *become* famous, I'll personally scrape it off."

Navigator gave his brother a deeply skeptical

look, and said, "Is that supposed to be a promise?"

"Trust me," Pilot said. "Don't worry. Everything will be fine."

Having heard those same words from his brother before, Navigator looked even more skeptical.

Pilot switched over to his smoothest voice. "It's what Grandpa would want, Nav. You know how he is. If he were here, he'd go in a minute!"

Navigator had to smile. "I have to admit, you're right about that. Less than a minute."

Pilot saw no problems. "By the time Grandpa gets home, we'll be back from our first trip. And we'll be all set to take him with us on the next one! He'll love it!"

After much more talk, Navigator agreed, and the twins started packing. For days, they loaded the ship with beds and pots and food from the house. They loaded hay from the barn. They loaded shovels and a thousand other things from the hardware side of the store. They loaded wagonloads from the shoe side. They loaded the miscellaneous stuff from the middle of the store.

With the last box aboard, Pilot stretched lazily. "We're all packed. Let's go fishing. We'll take off tomorrow."

"We have to decide what planet we start with," Navigator said. "I have to figure the course."

"I know," Pilot said. "Here, you take the fishing rods. I'll carry the bait."

"It takes time," Navigator said. "One little mistake and we could hit a sun."

"You're absolutely right," said Pilot. "Come on, we deserve a break. Let's try Indian Pond. I hear they're biting."

"I still think we ought to pick a planet *now*," Navigator said worriedly.

"Tomorrow," Pilot explained. "You worry too much. Fish today, pick a planet tomorrow."

CHAPTER 10

The Space Brothers Are Grounded

The next morning, while the brothers were eating breakfast in the old farmhouse kitchen, the mailman rang the doorbell.

"Morning, Vernon. Morning, Junior," Mr. Potts said.

(Mr. Potts had been delivering mail to the Smith farm since Grandpa was a boy, and he refused to call the brothers by their new names. "Pilot and Navigator, my foot!" he told his friends at the post office. "I called them Vernon and Junior when they were babies, and I'll call them Vernon and Junior now!")

"You're earlier than usual, Mr. Potts," Pilot told the mailman.

"Official business, Vernon," the mailman said.

"Special handling, rush delivery, registered letter for Vernon and Junior Smith. You both have to sign."

"What's it about?" Navigator asked.

"You'll never know till you sign," Mr. Potts said. "That's the law."

"Last time we signed for something, we got a spaceship," Pilot said.

"This time you get trouble," Mr. Potts said. "Letter's from the Commonwealth of Pennsylvania Revenue Department. They collect taxes. That's trouble." He kept a tight grasp on the letter until both brothers had signed.

When the mailman was gone, Pilot opened the letter. He read a few lines, then said, "Boy, is this stupid."

"What is?" Navigator asked.

"They got us mixed up with somebody else. I feel sorry for the guy this letter was really supposed to go to. This is weird." Pilot started reading out loud. "'Mr. Vernon Smith, Mr. Junior Smith.' They got our names right, but that's all. Listen. It says, 'This office is taking steps to collect the sales tax on your recent purchase of a vehicle.'"

Navigator interrupted. "Vehicle? We don't have a vehicle. . . . Is a bike a vehicle?"

Pilot shook his head and read from the letter. "'To avoid criminal charges, please send your check for one million, eight hundred thousand, nine hundred sixty dollars and twenty-nine cents.' That's some vehicle. Stupid letter." Pilot threw the letter into the wastebasket.

Navigator retrieved the letter and read it slowly. "It's for us, all right. This isn't about a bike. The vehicle they're talking about is the spaceship."

He started to read from the second page: "'Used vehicle: Length, seven hundred two feet . . . Type, space travel . . . Mileage, unknown . . . Make, unknown . . . Model, unknown.' Under Body Condition, it has things checked off. 'Scratches . . . Dents . . . Rust . . . Minor collision damage . . . Estimated value, thirty million dollars.' Oh, boy, here comes the worst," Navigator continued in a faint voice. "'Vehicle sales tax: one million eight hundred thousand . . . Penalty for late payment . . .'"

His face grim, Navigator looked up from the letter. "It's all worked out. Even the twenty-nine cents. This isn't a joke, Pilot. Mr. Potts was right. This is real trouble."

Pilot took the letter and looked at it closely. "It *looks* official," he said slowly. "All that gold printing. . . . Oh, well, why worry. They can't get money from us if we don't have it."

"Look at the end of the letter," Navigator said. "If we don't pay, they take the spaceship."

"They can't do that!" Pilot shouted. He grabbed the letter back and turned to the last page. "'Due to the large amount involved, a tax collector will visit you personally on July 27. If you fail to arrange payment by July 28, this department will be legally authorized to seize the spaceship and may sell it for taxes. Signed, Alton J. Weberschreber, Tax Collector Third Class.'" He looked up nervously. "What's today's date?"

Navigator peered at the wall calendar. "July 27! He's coming today!"

Pilot leaped to his feet. "Come on, let's go!"

"Go where?" Navigator asked.

"Out of here! Right now, before this tax bozo gets here!"

Navigator objected, but weakly. "We can't just run away. They'd catch us."

"Catch a spaceship? No way!"

"We'd be criminals, Pilot. We'd be stealing government property!"

"Read the letter again!" Pilot said. "It won't be government property till they seize it! And that's tomorrow!" He started to pull his brother toward the door. "Come on, this is our chance. We're as ready as we'll ever be! In the ship! Quick!"

"We don't have any clothes packed," Navigator said.

"Who cares? We'll get stuff on the next planet. Come on, will you *hurry*?" Pilot half-dragged his brother to the door and opened it.

The doorway was blocked by man who was

shaped like a pear. He had a shiny round head and a dead-serious look.

"Good morning, sirs. I believe I have some legal business with you," the man said. He spoke slowly, and sounded very important. "Am I interrupting something?"

"We were just leaving," Pilot said.

"Not in the spaceship, I hope." The voice was still slow and serious, but it had picked up a note of unfriendliness. "You weren't thinking of leaving in that, were you? Didn't you get the letter I sent?"

He didn't wait for an answer but stepped into the house and closed the door behind him. Once inside, he took a hard look at the brothers. "Are you Vernon and Junior Smith?" he asked.

Vernon looked at the signature on the letter. "Are you this tax collector?"

"Tax collector third class, I am proud to say. You may call me Mr. Weberschreber. Or Alton, if you prefer a friendlier approach." He sounded as friendly as a stone.

The twins glanced at each other and exchanged a silent message: *No way. We're never going to call this guy by his first name.*

Fumbling in his briefcase, Alton J. Weberschreber said, "Where was I? Oh, yes. You really *are* Vernon and Junior Smith?"

The twins admitted they were.

"I had to ask," the tax collector said. "You're so

much younger than the suspects I usually deal with. Most of them are lawyers or professional criminals. Or both."

"What's that?" Pilot objected. "Are you saying we're *suspects*?"

Alton J. Weberschreber ignored Pilot's question, and shook his round head. "But you—how old are you, thirteen? With all your life ahead of you, why would you take up a career of criminal tax evasion?"

The twins objected loudly: "WE DIDN'T! WHO ARE YOU CALLING CRIMINALS! ARE YOU CRAZY? WHAT ARE YOU TALKING ABOUT?"

Alton J. Weberschreber didn't seem to hear a word. He dug into his briefcase, came up with crumpled papers, and handed one to each of the boys. "I recommend this. It is the only way to take care of your debt without making terrible trouble for yourself."

"You mean we don't have to pay?" Vernon asked.

"It's not quite as simple as that," Alton J. Weberschreber said solemnly. "Those legal papers tell you the tax collection division is taking over the spaceship. Step one, we own it; step two, we auction it off; step three, you don't have to pay. Simple and easy. All you have to do is agree."

Neither twin reacted, so Alton explained. "That's how the tax collection division works. We have the most efficient system in the entire Pennsylvania government. We don't waste time suing people to get them to give us what we want. We just mail them a letter and take it." Alton made all that sound very ordinary.

The boys released a storm of protest: "YOU CAN'T DO THIS. IT'S OUR SHIP! WE DON'T OWE ANY SALES TAX! WHAT ARE YOU, A PIRATE? YOU'RE NOT EFFICIENT, YOU'RE A THIEF!" And so on.

Alton J. Weberschreber waited until the twins ran down. Then he shook his head and—in the same serious, boring voice—said, "Terrible, the way our schools fail to teach government rules and regulations. Young people seldom appreciate it, but government rules and regulations are the American way! Government rules and regulations preserve civilization as we know it! I am proud to be an enforcer of my government's rules and regulations!"

Alton J. Weberschreber paused to let the boys see what a proud tax collector looked like. "Vernon and Junior, in Pennsylvania, one of the government's strictest rules is, you must pay taxes."

"We know that," Pilot said quickly.

Alton J. Weberschreber pulled in his stomach, threw back his shoulders, thrust out his chin, and said loudly, "As tax collector third class for North-central Pennsylvania, it is my duty, under

Regulation 3343-dash-B, to collect one million, eight hundred thousand, nine hundred sixty dollars and twenty-nine cents. Sales tax. Calculated according to Regulation B998-dash-OP3, the amount you owe will increase one-point-three-nine percent every day until—"

Navigator interrupted to demand, "Why should we pay a sales tax when we didn't *buy* anything?"

Alton droned on as if nobody had said a word, "Furthermore, Regulation J930, paragraph 3, frowns on keeping a vehicle hidden from view in your backyard. It was foolish of you to try to keep it secret. The tax collection division that I am proud to belong to has a network of public-spirited citizens who report anybody who suddenly looks rich. I have known about the spaceship for quite a while."

"So what?" Pilot cried. "It's never been a secret!"

Alton didn't pause but rolled on, "Your spaceship is worth a great deal of money. So you must have paid a great deal of money for it." He allowed just a hint of a smile to flicker. "And you haven't paid the sales tax on that money!"

"We don't know anything about taxes on spaceships," Navigator said.

"Ignorance is no excuse," said Alton J. Weberschreber. "Cars, planes, spaceships—all vehicles are the same. When you buy one, you pay the sales tax immediately."

"Sorry to disappoint you," Navigator said. "But we didn't buy the spaceship."

Alton J. Weberschreber almost chuckled. His

almost-chuckle had no humor in it at all. "Oh? I suppose you found it."

"It sort of found us," Navigator explained. "One morning it was just here. A deliveryman brought it."

"How nice of him," Alton J. Weberschreber said in a fifty/fifty mixture of monotony and sarcasm. "And how much did you pay for this service?"

Pilot was feeling uncomfortable. "Nothing. It was all paid for. In advance."

"And who paid for it?" the tax collector asked, in a way that made it clear that he wasn't about to believe a word.

"We don't know anything about that," Pilot said, feeling trapped in a story that was beginning to sound far-fetched even to him. "The deliveryman didn't know either."

Alton J.Weberschreber shook his shiny, round head. "It is my duty to ask for any proof of ownership you might have."

"Right here!" Navigator opened the drawer where Grandpa kept his important papers and took out the metal paper the deliveryman had left. "Look at this!"

Alton J. Weberschreber read the metal paper slowly. He sighed. "We tax collectors hear a lot of wild stories. People will say anything to get out of paying taxes. I don't mind. The stories can be interesting, if you like fantasy. But *this*!"

He took a deep breath, and his face turned

purple with indignation. "The Anytime/Anywhere Spaceship Delivery Company? This is the wildest yet. This insults the intelligence of honest tax collectors everywhere!"

Alton J. Weberschreber gripped the metal paper with his fingertips and tried to tear it in half. It wouldn't tear. He gripped it in both hands and tried again. He couldn't rip it. Giving up, he crumpled it angrily into a tight ball and tossed it toward the brothers. It flattened out in the air. Navigator reached out and caught it as it floated by. There wasn't a wrinkle in it; the metal paper was smooth as new.

"It isn't fake," Navigator said. "We got it from the deliveryman."

"Yes, well, I suppose you can try getting the jury to swallow that one," said Alton J. Weberschreber.

"What jury?" the brothers exclaimed together.

"The one at your trial, of course," Alton J. Weberschreber said. "Evading taxes is a serious crime. Did I mention that? Regulation 699-dash-Section C, paragraph 3."

"You mean we could go to *jail*?" Navigator asked.

"That is most likely," Alton J. Weberschreber said. "Unless the jury believes your incredible story."

"How long?" Navigator said with a gulp.

"Government regulations set the limit at fifteen years," said Alton J. Weberschreber solemnly. "I thought that was low, but they didn't bother to consult me. If I were you, I'd count on ten years. Possibly five—no—million-dollar tax evaders get more than five years. Ten years is safe."

The brothers were chilled with sudden fear.

"Unless. . . ." Alton J. Weberschreber said.

"Unless *what?*" the brothers cried.

"Well, you *could* sign those papers I gave you," Alton J. Weberschreber said.

"What then?" Pilot asked.

"Then the tax collection division could take care of everything smoothly, using the efficient method I explained. You wouldn't owe a penny! Or go to jail! Or have all the trouble that came with this spaceship! Surely, that should make you happy," the tax collector said with a hint of a smile.

"Not a chance!" Pilot said.

"I don't think we'd be happy at all," Navigator said.

For the first time, Alton smiled a real smile. It was the kind of smile a shark smiles while eating dinner. "I understand. You'd rather wait ten years in jail before you get to ride in a spaceship. Well, if that's your decision." He picked up the papers from the table.

"Let's see those!" Pilot said as he snatched the papers out of Alton J. Weberschreber's hand.

Alton J. Weberschreber smiled once more. It was the kind of smile a shark smiles *after* dinner.

"You don't have to decide right now. You may sign the papers tonight, if you prefer. I'll drop by and pick them up in the morning."

"Don't be too sure," Pilot said angrily.

"Personally, I will not object strongly if you don't sign," Alton J. Weberschreber said solemnly, as he turned to leave. "Then you'll have ten years to wish you hadn't put a hardworking tax collector to all this trouble."

As he was stepping out the door, he turned back to the brothers. "I wouldn't want any harm to come to the spaceship. So I'll take care of it for a while."

"What do you mean, take care of it?" Pilot demanded.

"I mean I'll watch over it," Alton J. Weberschreber explained. "Make sure nobody damages it."

"We wouldn't damage the spaceship!" Navigator said. "It belongs to us!"

"But you might try to fly it away," said Alton J. Weberschreber. "Then we'd never collect the taxes you owe. And I might never become tax collector second class—maybe even first. That would be *serious* damage."

"How do you think you're going to keep us out of our spaceship?" Pilot asked in a challenging tone.

"I'll guard the entrance," the tax collector said.

"Suppose we walk up the stairs," Pilot said. "What are you going to do, shoot us?"

"Let me explain Government Regulation 1002-

dash-P34," Alton J. Weberschreber said. "It is against the law to interfere with a tax collector performing his duty."

He opened his coat to show a mean-looking gun in a shoulder holster. "Tax collectors are required to carry a gun. I've never used it, but if it was my sad duty, I would have no choice, would I?"

"You have no right to take over our spaceship now!" Navigator said hotly. "The letter said you wouldn't take it till tomorrow!"

"It may *look* as if I am taking over the spaceship now," said Alton J. Weberschreber, "but I am merely safeguarding future government property. You won't be using the spaceship, gentlemen. Consider yourselves grounded."

CHAPTER 11

The Spaceship Is Captured

Pilot paced up and down the kitchen floor like a wildcat in a cage. "Just when things were looking great—blooey!" He looked to the ceiling and demanded an answer: "Why me? That's what I want to know. Why me?"

Navigator was sitting at the kitchen table, wishing his brother wouldn't talk so loud. "Why you? What's that supposed to mean?" he asked.

Pilot kept pacing as he answered, "Why does my spaceship have to get grounded?"

"It's my spaceship too," Navigator pointed out.

"It *was* your spaceship. As long as this stupid tax collector—what's his name?"

"Alton J. Weberschreber," Navigator replied.

"That's right! What kind of fishy name is that?" demanded Pilot. "He probably made it up! Anyway, as long as whatshisname is inside the spaceship, and we're outside—it isn't our spaceship anymore."

"Quit complaining. Think about getting it back," Navigator said mildly.

"Easy to say," Pilot said. "Whatshisname has the stairs up, and he's sitting in the doorway like a gorilla, watching TV."

"How do you know?" Navigator asked.

Pilot answered, "Every time I look out my window, he's watching the news."

"I think I'll take a peek," said Navigator, and went upstairs.

A minute later, he called down in a loud whisper, "Pilot! Come here!"

Pilot started up the stairs two at a time. Navigator whispered a loud, *Shhh!*

Pilot tiptoed the rest of the way. "What's going on?" he whispered.

Navigator was peeking out his bedroom window. "I can't figure out what he's doing," he said, pointing down the length of the spaceship.

Pilot saw the tax collector standing in the spaceship's main entrance. By his feet a little portable TV was turned on, but he wasn't watching it. He was reading out loud from a notebook.

"Who's he talking to?" Pilot whispered.

"Himself," Navigator whispered back. "Listen."

The brothers could just make out what Alton J. Weberschreber was saying: "Until just a few hours ago, this spaceship was being kept secret by two people who claimed to own it. This is a criminal violation of Regulation J930 paragraph 3. Then, just as they were planning to. . . . "

Alton J. Weberschreber stopped, shook his head, wrote something in the notebook, and started again. "They were conspiring to sneak the ship away and cheat the state out of nearly two million dollars in sales tax—a crime under Regulation 3343-dash-B."

Alton J. Weberschreber stopped, nodded, wrote a few words in the notebook, and continued. "To make sure the criminals would not tamper with the ship, I personally stood guard. . . . "

"Has he gone crazy?" Navigator whispered.

"He knows what he's doing," Pilot whispered back. "He's practicing for the TV news."

"He's going to tell them we're criminals?" In his excitement, Navigator spoke out loud.

Putting his hand over his brother's mouth, Pilot whispered, "Quiet! Do you want him to find out that we're watching?"

Navigator whispered furiously, "He can't say that stuff about us on TV!"

"He'll say it unless we do something," Pilot said. "Come on down to the kitchen."

As they tiptoed down the stairs, the tax collector

was still talking. The last thing they heard him say was, "The criminals threatened to attack, but I held them off."

"What a liar!" Pilot said.

"Forget what he says," Navigator told his brother. "Think about where he *is*."

"I know where he is," Pilot said sourly. "He's in our ship."

"If only there was some way to get him out," Navigator said.

"Hmmm," said Pilot.

CHAPTER 12

The Space Brothers Hatch a Plan

"Hmmm, what?" Navigator said.

Pilot squinted his eyes and sat as still as a rock. Navigator knew that look. No use talking to his brother until it changed. He waited.

Minutes later, Pilot opened his eyes wide, stood up, and said, "Yes! He'll move for *that*!"

"Move for what?" Navigator asked.

"We're all right now!" Pilot exclaimed. "I know it'll work!"

"Are you going to let me in on this?" Navigator asked quietly. "Or would you rather be called Vernon?"

Pilot took a deep breath, then started out by saying, "It's really a simple plan."

When Pilot finished explaining, Navigator said, "I don't know. What if it goes wrong?"

"Got a better idea?" Pilot asked.

Navigator had to admit he didn't. He thought for a while. "It can't get us into any more trouble than we're in now. . . . I guess we better try it."

"Attaboy!" Pilot said. "I'll call the TV station now!"

"There's just one more thing we ought to do first," said Navigator.

"What one thing?" Pilot asked impatiently.

"We need to time everything just right. We need to know *his* plan."

"How do you think we can get that?" asked Pilot.

"We just have to do a little spying," Navigator explained. "Why don't you walk over there and see what you can find out?"

"I came up with the plan, didn't I?" Pilot replied. "Planners don't spy. They stay at headquarters."

"Oh, all right," said Navigator, "I'll be the spy."

"Look innocent," said Pilot.

Navigator rolled his eyes. Just the same, he tried whistling innocently as he strolled out to the spaceship.

Standing on the ground below the main entrance, he called up to Alton J. Weberschreber, "Hi! How are you doing?"

Alton growled. (He even made a growl sound dull.) "Get away from the ship."

"I can't do anything down here. I just wanted to say—no hard feelings," said Navigator. "You're just doing your duty."

Alton wasn't interested. "Fine, you've said it. Now get away, boy. I'm busy with important government business."

"Sure thing," Navigator answered. "By the way, would you like some coffee? Or iced tea?"

"Nice try," Alton J. Weberschreber said with a sneer. (He could sneer boringly, too.) "I lower the steps, then you sneak into the ship. Right? Well, let me tell you, my boy, these steps stay up until ten tomorrow morning."

"What happens then?" Navigator asked.

"Why, your spaceship will be on TV," Alton said. "All the TV networks will be here. And I'm going to tell them about you two. Any objections?"

"No, no, that's your job," said Navigator. "See you tomorrow morning. . . . Did you say ten o'clock?"

"That's right," said Alton J. Weberschreber. "Now get away from this future government property."

"Just trying to be neighborly," Navigator said calmly, and strolled slowly to the house. Back inside, he gave his brother a big smile. "The TV networks are coming at ten in the morning! We have to move fast!"

"Okay," Pilot said. "Here it goes with the local

news. Wish me luck." He picked up the phone and dialed. "Hello, is this *Channel 7 News*? This is Pilot—I mean, this is Vernon Smith. From Whipple Crossing. The Famous Smith Brothers Store? Oh, you remember the sign?" He smiled at his brother triumphantly. His look said, I told you so.

"Good," Pilot continued. "Well, I'm one of the Smith brothers, and I have a news story for you . . . No. This isn't about the store, nothing like that. This is national news. . . . Well, I think it's national because all the networks will be here at ten tomorrow morning. They didn't invite you, huh? Man, that's rotten. Would you like to beat them all to the story tonight?"

While Pilot talked, Navigator walked nervously from room to room, killing time by filling his pockets. Toothbrushes, candy bars, comic books, anything that caught his eye. He noticed the sheet of metal paper the deliveryman had given them and absentmindedly kept trying to fold it to pocket size. But it kept opening up, so he slipped it, flat, inside his shirt, and ambled on.

Pilot went on talking to *Channel 7 News* for what seemed like forever. Finally, though, he ran out of words. The last thing he said before hanging up was, "Cool! We'll be waiting on the porch!"

CHAPTER 13

Outwitting Alton

Behind the house, Alton J. Weberschreber sleepily guarded the spaceship. On the front porch, the brothers watched the road.

It was dusk when a television news truck boomed up Smith Lane and stopped in front of the farmhouse.

A crowd of people, all wearing sweaters, jumped out of the news truck. They carried big lights, microphones, cameras, and black boxes with handles. Like a colony of oversize ants, the sweater people ran in twenty different directions at once.

While the confusion was at its height, Navigator dashed into the house, out the back door, and straight to the spot below the spaceship entrance.

"Hey, Alton!" Navigator shouted. "Turn on the TV news! Hurry!"

Alton J. Weberschreber had been dozing in the spaceship doorway. Now he stood up. "What do you want?" he asked.

"There's a Channel 7 news truck out front!" Navigator cried. "Better tune in! Channel 7!" He ran into the house, locked the back door, and rejoined his brother on the front porch.

He got there just in time to watch the last person step out of the truck. This was a handsome man, wearing a raincoat and carrying nothing, who walked slowly to the bottom of the porch steps.

Ignoring the cameras, Raincoat turned to the Sweaters and asked, "How do I look?"

A sweater girl carrying a black make-up box ran a comb through his hair and patted his nose with a makeup pad. "Perfect," she said seriously.

"I know," Raincoat said. He turned to the crowd of sweater people, looked them over carefully, frowned to show he wasn't quite satisfied, and said, "Ready?"

"All ready, Don," the sweater people answered brightly.

"Here we go," Raincoat said. His frown disappeared. He beamed a big smile at the cameras. "Good evening, ladies and gentlemen. This is your guaranteed-truthful television news reporter, Don Prefer, with an exclusive live report on a story of world importance. It's about our state government's latest idea—if you don't have a spaceship, steal one!"

The brothers heard a far-off shout of surprise. It was Alton J. Weberschreber. Raincoat didn't notice.

Raincoat kept smiling and talking. "Yesterday, Whipple Crossing, Pennsylvania, population three hundred and ninety-three, was a village the world had never heard of. Tonight, the place becomes forever famous as the home of a scientific marvel and of a pair of teenage twins named Smith.

"Because of these boys, the most advanced spaceship the world has ever seen is parked on the Smith farm. No other country in the world has anything like it. This amazing ship is literally centuries ahead of its time."

Raincoat continued. "What is the government of Pennsylvania doing about this? Are they honoring the Smith boys? Oh, no. They plan to seize the spaceship, sell it to enrich the bloated Pennsylvania treasury, and put the Smith boys in jail!"

The brothers heard another shout from Alton J. Weberschreber. He sounded furious. He also sounded closer.

Raincoat heard it, too, and looked puzzled. But he ignored the noise and walked up to the brothers. Holding a microphone toward them, he said, "Vernon and Junior Smith, please tell the television audience—how did this spaceship get here?"

"It was delivered here, where we live," Navigator replied.

Raincoat asked, "And who owns the spaceship?"

"We do," Pilot said. "Both of us. We didn't buy it, but we own it."

"And we can prove it," Navigator said.

There was another shout from Alton. He sounded outraged. The brothers heard him try to pull the back door open. He pulled so hard, the whole house rattled. They could hear him starting around the house, his feet pounding like wild horses.

Pilot spoke quickly. "I guess you want to know why the government thinks it can just take our spaceship?"

"I do, and so does the television audience," said Raincoat.

Pilot pointed to the corner of the house and said loudly, "Well, if you'll just point your camera that way, you'll see the man who knows the answer."

Alton J. Weberschreber swung around the end of the house like a charging bull. The lights blinded him, and he stopped. "Not now!" he shouted. "This is against regulations! Absolutely no TV news today! Come back tomorrow morning!"

The television news crew crowded around Alton. They shone lights in his eyes and held microphones to his face. Raincoat fired questions at him without giving him a chance to speak. Alton spouted regulation numbers. Raincoat talked louder.

Quietly, the brothers stepped into the house and locked the front door. On tiptoe, they crossed to the back door and unlocked it. Silently, they stepped outside. Hopefully, they looked down the length of the ship.

Oh, thrilling! Oh, glorious! Oh joyful sight! In his haste to reach the TV cameras, Alton J. Weberschreber had left the stairway down!

The brothers ran with every bit of speed they could find, laughing wildly all the way.

In twenty seconds they had reached the bottom of the steps.

In thirty seconds they were inside the spaceship.

In forty seconds they had the stairs pulled up and out of reach.

In fifty seconds, they had the door locked and sealed.

In sixty seconds, they were seated in the control room.

"Takeoff time!" Pilot said, holding his fingers above the buttons. "Ready?"

"No, I'm not ready!" Navigator said. "We need to pick a planet! I have to compute a course! I need some time!"

They heard a wild yell in the distance. From the sound, it might have been Alton—or possibly an angry bear.

"How much time?" snapped Pilot.

"Fifteen minutes!"

They heard a wild yell from outside. It sounded like an angry elephant, but looking out the porthole, the brothers saw Alton J. Weberschreber on the ground below the control room. Sweaters surrounded him with lights and microphones. Raincoat was pouring questions in his ear. Alton didn't look bored anymore; his face was red and his eyes glared with a color never seen before.

"Come out of there, or I'll wreck the ship!" he roared.

"We don't *have* fifteen minutes," Pilot said. "Thinker!"

"Wait a minute!" Navigator exclaimed.

"Can't wait!" Pilot said. "Thinker!"

"My hearing is better than yours," Thinker answered sulkily. "You don't have to shout."

"At least let me talk to him," said Navigator. "It, I mean. Sorry about that, Thinker."

"That's quite all right, Navigator," Thinker said. "I'll gladly talk to you any time."

"Quiet, both of you," Pilot shouted. "We're out of time. Thinker!"

"I told you, I can hear," Thinker said, sounding very annoyed.

Pilot said, "Do you have any planets in your memory?"

"I always keep a few handy," Thinker replied. "Right now, let me see—three thousand, one hundred and twelve planets, ready on a moment's notice. Why do you want to know?"

"I want you to pick a planet and give us a

course," Pilot said. "Any planet! Now!"

"If I must," Thinker said wearily. "What type?"

"What do you mean, what type?" Pilot snapped.

"What type of planet do you want?" Thinker replied, sounding bored. "Bone-dry Mercury type? Toxic-air type, like Saturn? Covered with jagged boulders, like some I know?"

"No, dummy! A planet with good air! And good water like we have! Pick one! Hurry!"

"Anything else you want to find on the planet I select?" Thinker sounded bored.

"A level place to land!" Pilot snapped. "You know what we need! Air, water, landing! And no weird aliens! Got that? Come on! We're out of time!"

"Wait a second!" Navigator exclaimed.

They heard a gunshot and felt a bullet bang on the outside of the ship.

"Pick a planet!" Pilot shouted. "That's an order! No more delay!"

"I need to talk to Thinker!" Navigator shouted.

"May I make a suggestion?" Thinker asked.

They felt three more bullets hit. On the ground below the control room, Alton threw the driver out of the television truck and started to turn it toward the spaceship. For a pear-shaped guy, he was turning out to be pretty tough. Faintly, they heard him shout, "Out of my way! I'm going to ram!"

"No advice! No suggestions!" Pilot snapped. "Just do it!"

"Planet with good air, water, and landing space chosen, Pilot," Thinker said in a resentful tone. "Following your instructions, Pilot. Course computed, Pilot. Ready for takeoff, Pilot."

Pilot began pressing buttons.

The people on the ground outside the spaceship remembered different things about the next minute. Some remembered the spaceship tilting up and pointing at the sky. Some remembered a glow as bright as the sun. Some remembered the ground shaking like a major earthquake.

But they all shared the same memory of the bullhorn voice from the spaceship. It was clearly the voice of a machine. A large, powerful, unfriendly machine. Very slowly and distinctly, it said: "WARNING. WARNING. IN FORTY-THREE SECONDS, ALL PERSONS WITHIN ONE HUNDRED YARDS OF THIS SPACESHIP WILL BE TURNED INTO WET, RED DUST. THIS IS YOUR ONLY WARNING. ALL PERSONS WILL BE WET, RED DUST IN FORTY SECONDS . . . THIRTY-NINE SECONDS . . . THIRTY-EIGHT SECONDS . . . "

You have never seen anybody run as fast as those television news people did. By the time the voice reached "FIVE SECONDS," most of them were scrunched down on the other side of the house, trying to hide behind one another.

Alton was the last to run. At "FOUR

SECONDS," he turned as he ran, fired one last shot at the spaceship, and leaped over a fence into a ditch full of muddy water.

The last thing the voice said was, "THREE SECONDS. THANK YOU FOR VISITING THE FAMOUS SPACE BROTHERS ORIGINAL TRADING POST. GOOD-BYE, AND HAVE A NICE DAY."

There was a sound. It was too violent to describe in words. Some people said afterward that it reminded them of a giant tearing a large mountain to pieces. But since very few of them had actually heard any mountains being torn to pieces, they may have been mistaken. After a long minute, the sound faded away, and everything was silent.

One by one, the TV people got up and began to peek around the corner of the house to see what had happened. Their floodlights showed them a round patch of flattened hay about the size of a hockey rink. They saw a thick cloud of green smoke drifting upward. They smelled a strong odor of peanut butter mixed with apples and firecrackers.

There was no sign of the spaceship.

For a while, everyone just wandered around without saying a word. Raincoat walked through the twins' old home. On the kitchen table, he found a note. It was written on the back of the paper Alton J. Weberschreber had tried to get the brothers to sign. Calling his crew together, Raincoat read the note to the camera:

> Dear Grandpa,
>
> Sorry, but a big emergency landed and we have to leave in a hurry. Mr. Prefer from Channel 7 can explain.
>
> Don't worry about us! I know all about flying a spaceship now! (Pilot put that in.)
>
> No matter what the tax collector says, we never bought the ship. (Navigator added that.)
>
> Don't worry about the stuff we took from the store. We'll put it all back as soon as we do some trading.
>
> Love,
> Pilot and Navigator
> (Vernon and Junior)
>
> P.S. Have a good time at the South Pole.

Raincoat paused dramatically. "Because of the runaway greed of a Pennsylvania tax collector, an incredibly advanced spaceship has left our state and gone to an unknown part of the universe. It took with it the owners, a remarkable pair of teenage twins. The first of many questions the world will demand answers to is: Where are they now?"

At that moment, the Space Brothers were wondering the same thing.

CHAPTER 14

First Flight of the Famous Space Brothers Original Trading Post

From where the brothers sat in the control room, the takeoff was quite interesting.

When Pilot heard the announcement that scared everybody away from the spaceship, he was delighted. "Hey! That'll get rid of that creep!"

When Navigator heard the announcement, he was horrified. "Hold it! We don't want to hurt anybody! Stop right now!"

Thinker answered, "Oh, there's really no danger. I just said that to get their attention. Look, even that madman who was shooting at us is running away."

"You mean you made that up?" Navigator asked.

"I thought it was a nice touch," Thinker said

smugly. "When you've seen as many takeoffs as I have, they get boring. I like to add a little excitement when I can."

Pilot really loved Thinker's little joke, but he wanted to make sure the robot understood who was in charge. "Listen, you!" he shouted. "I want you to follow orders! I don't want you doing any old thing that comes to mind!"

"I don't have a *mind*," Thinker said with a sneer in its voice. "We Post-Electronic Thinking Systems have nothing in common with what persons like you call a mind."

"Don't get smart with me," Pilot said angrily. "Get it straight! Obey orders, or I'll unplug you!"

"I did exactly what you told me to do," Thinker said. "In about five seconds, we'll be heading straight for the exact planet you ordered."

"Good thing," Pilot said.

"I hope you like it," Thinker said.

"What's that supposed to mean?" Pilot said.

Before Thinker could answer, Alton's last bullet banged against the spaceship.

The brothers took a deep breath. Thinker said, "Another day, another takeoff."

The control-room windows turned solid black. The stars disappeared.

The engine gave a deep *Blatt!* The brothers didn't hear or feel anything, so they sat and waited.

"Didn't I tell you takeoffs were boring?" Thinker said.

After waiting a few minutes more, Navigator asked, "When do we take off?"

"We took off a little while ago," Thinker said.

The brothers looked out the window. It had turned clear. As they stared, the moon slid by.

"Incredible!" Navigator said.

"Oh, that's nothing for this spaceship," Thinker said. "It's a very advanced model."

"What now?" Navigator said.

"What now? Nothing," Thinker replied. "There's nothing for you to do. Watch the stars until we arrive at the planet Pilot ordered."

"That's what I like to hear," Pilot said. "You're catching on, Thinker." He stretched out in his pilot's chair and put his feet upon the control board. "How soon do we get there?"

Thinker replied calmly, "At maximum standard speed, a little over fourteen years."

Pilot's feet crashed to the floor. "Cut the kidding," he said.

"I certainly am not kidding," Thinker replied. "The engine is now at full standard power, which should get us there in—let me think a moment— fourteen years, one week, and six days."

"Did . . . you . . . say . . . fourteen . . . years?" Pilot squeezed out the words as if they hurt his throat.

"And one week and six days," Thinker said. "Not exact, but close."

Pilot got his voice back and screamed, "You idiot! You maniac! Are you trying to kill us?"

Thinker answered in its sweetest, most annoying voice, "Didn't you order me to pick one of the planets in my memory?"

Pilot glared.

Thinker said, "Didn't Navigator tell you not to give that order?"

Pilot began to breathe heavily.

Thinker said, "Didn't I give you a choice of planets? And didn't you turn those down and tell me to pick a planet with good air and good water and a big level space to land? And no weird aliens? And keep my suggestions to myself?"

Pilot bared his teeth in a snarl.

Thinker said, "Well, that's where we're going. To the only planet in my memory that could fill your order exactly."

Pilot stood up and took a step toward Thinker. His fingers were curved like claws.

"Hands off, Pilot!" Navigator said. "You can argue, but that's all! You promised!"

"Actually, it's not as bad as it sounds," Thinker said.

Pilot's eyes glared redly, but he stood still.

"In fact, it's just my little joke," Thinker said nervously.

"I told you to obey orders!" Pilot told Thinker.

Navigator put his arm around his brother's shoulder and walked him to one of the large windows. The stars looked like Christmas tree lights but bigger. "I don't think this is serious," he said. "You heard—it's a joke."

"I heard fourteen years!" Pilot said. "We'll starve before we get there!" He leaned his forehead against the glass.

"You watch the stars for a while," Navigator said in a soothing voice. "I'll be back as soon as I straighten this out with Thinker."

Navigator didn't want his brother to hear him say anything nice to Thinker, so he kept his voice to a whisper when he said, "That was amazing, Thinker."

"It was?" Thinker said, sounding surprised.

"Completely amazing," Navigator said. "You really impressed me."

"Why, thank you, Navigator," Thinker said, sounding delighted. "Just what was it that you liked?"

"Everything!" said Navigator. "The whole way you picked a planet and computed a course and got us launched. All in a few seconds. I could never hope to do that."

"Oh, you'll get faster with practice," Thinker said. He sounded very self-satisfied.

"Not as fast as you, Thinker," said Navigator.

"Of course not," Thinker said. "But maybe I can

give you some tips." He sounded very self-important.

"That would be wonderful!" Navigator said. He looked down at the floor as if he were embarrassed. "Sorry Pilot got so upset," he said.

"He can't take a joke, can he?" said Thinker.

"Fourteen years in space isn't exactly a joke," Navigator said. "I know we can pick another planet to go to. But first we have to stop the ship in space, and that's no joke, either."

"You think I was wrong, don't you?" Thinker said sadly.

"Well, you could have given Pilot the bad news without insisting it was his fault," Navigator said.

"But the bad news doesn't have to be bad!" Thinker said. "That's the joke!"

"What do you mean?" Navigator asked.

"Do you remember what Einstein said about the speed limit?" Thinker asked.

Navigator thought for a moment and said, "You mean the speed of light?" he asked. "Nothing is allowed to go faster than the speed of light?"

"Exactly!" Thinker said. "Einstein said it was impossible."

"The instruction books for the spaceship say it's impossible, too," Navigator said. "Are you saying they're wrong?"

"Oh, it's not in the instruction books," Thinker said. "The Fast Drive discovery was made after this ship was built."

"What's the Fast Drive discovery?" Navigator asked.

"Well, it's what Einstein was getting around to," Thinker said. "He was right, you can never go exactly the speed of light. But you *can* go faster. Isn't that neat?"

"I guess it's neat if you know how," Navigator said. "*We* sure don't."

"I do," Thinker said happily. "Since it wasn't in the instruction books, they put it in my memory."

"I don't know," Navigator said. "Faster than light . . . I'm not sure I want to try that."

Thinker said, "Well, how much time do you want to spend getting to the planet Pilot insisted on—fourteen years or fourteen minutes?"

Navigator said, "Fourteen *minutes*? Really?"

Thinker said, "It doesn't matter how far we go; it's always fourteen minutes. Now, why don't you and Pilot sit down and buckle up? I'll show you."

Navigator had to do some fancy talking to get Pilot to cool down and listen. He had to do more to get Pilot to sit down and buckle up.

"This better be good, Thinker," Pilot growled.

"You worry too much," Thinker said sweetly. "Everybody ready? Seat belts fastened? Very well, Pilot, Fast Drive is enabled. Full speed ahead."

Pilot pressed Button 912, Button 499, and Button 3.

The windows went black. The lights went out.

All the normal hums and creaks that a spaceship makes were silenced.

"Nothing to worry about," Thinker said. "That always happens on Fast Drive."

"How do we know when fourteen minutes are up?" Pilot said. "I can't even see my watch."

"Would you like to take a little nap?" Thinker said. "That's what most pilots do during Fast Drive. I'll wake you just before we get there."

"I'll stay awake," Pilot said grimly.

"I think I will too," said Navigator.

"I could play some music that takes fourteen minutes," Thinker offered.

"No music," Pilot said with a growl.

"Music is nice . . . but I don't think I'd enjoy it right now," Navigator said.

When everything is black and silent, fourteen minutes seems forever. Just as Navigator was about to ask "How long?" for the tenth time—and Pilot was about to explode—Thinker said, "Here we go on our tour of a planet with good air, good water, lots and lots of level space for landing, and not a single weird alien in sight. Are you ready for this?"

The lights went on, the windows turned clear, and the hums and creaks came back.

Straight ahead of the spaceship was a new world. The part lighted by the sun was a blue crescent. The rest was in shadow and almost invisible. The brothers stared and gasped.

Navigator exclaimed, "Amazing, Thinker! All that distance and you got a bull's-eye! Great navigating!"

"We thinking systems are famed for our accuracy," Thinker said smugly.

Pilot started turning the ship to circle the planet. In a cheerful voice, he said, "Thinker, I have to admit, you may not be so bad after all."

Thinker made a small, disrespectful noise.

CHAPTER 15

The Trouble with People

As Pilot started the first long curve toward the blue edge of the planet, he asked, "How come all the blue?"

"Don't you know the ocean when you see it?" Thinker replied. "The big white streaks are clouds; the little ones are waves."

Pilot completed the first high circle around the planet and swung the ship sharply lower. "I don't believe this," he said.

"What's the matter?" Navigator asked.

Pilot didn't answer, but only muttered darkly to himself.

Navigator walked to the main viewing window and looked down at the expanse of blue ocean. "I hope the water's warm. Looks like good swimming."

"You think it's nice, huh?" Pilot said. "Well, we've been all the way around this planet twice. Know how much land I saw?"

"How much?" Navigator said.

"None. It's all water."

"Ah, you must have missed some islands," Navigator said skeptically.

"Not a chance," said Pilot. "I covered every inch. No islands. No rocks. No sandbars. Nothing but water."

"Thinker," Pilot said in an I-can't-believe-this voice. "This is your idea of a planet? A big, fat ball of water with no land?"

"Actually, Pilot," Thinker replied, "there's plenty of land; you just can't see it. It's covered with water. Besides, you never mentioned land. You ordered only good air, good water, and a level place for the spaceship to land."

"Where?" Pilot objected. "No runways, no control towers—where are we supposed to land?"

"This planet has several hundred million square miles of ocean, Pilot. Sweet, fresh water, by the way, excellent for drinking. And it's all level! Think of it as one big runway. You may land anywhere," Thinker said. "Please note that your order is now completely filled."

Slouched in his control seat, Pilot had a little

daydream. In it, he disassembled Thinker into thousands of tiny parts, then lost most of them. After enjoying the dream for a few seconds, he snapped back to real life.

Giving Thinker a sour look, he said, "Well, it's a planet. Might as well see what it's like. All hands fasten life preservers! Prepare for ocean landing!"

Pilot began the elaborate routine of slowing the spaceship down to a safe speed as it passed through the stratosphere and then into the atmosphere. This required him to move eighty controls, each move at an exact time. In the middle of this, Pilot tossed a question over his shoulder: "Hey, Thinker, where do they live? In underwater domes?"

"Where do *who* live?" Thinker asked innocently.

"The people! Where do the *people* live?" Pilot demanded. "Boy, you're dense today."

Thinker replied in a voice as sweet as syrup, "People? What people are those?"

Pilot froze in his seat. "Don't play games, Thinker. You know what people! The people on this planet!"

"If you required a planet with people, you should have said so while you were shouting orders, Pilot," Thinker said. "I am programmed to obey your orders, and I did. In every detail. To the letter. Surely, you are not going to criticize me for doing my duty perfectly."

Pilot shook the wheel so hard he almost flipped the ship upside down. In a voice of pure outrage, he shrieked, "DO YOU MEAN—ARE YOU SERIOUS—ARE THERE PEOPLE ON THIS PLANET OR NOT?"

"The old records do not show any people on the planet since a spaceship landed here, floated for a time, and finally sank," Thinker replied.

"What? You brought us to planet where spaceships *sink*?" Pilot said with a squawk.

"Only one spaceship," Thinker replied breezily. "If you don't bungle the landing, there should be nothing to worry about, Pilot."

Navigator interrupted. "What happened to the people? The crew of the ship, I mean."

"The old records don't say," Thinker said. "Of course, those records were kept on those primitive—what do you call them?—oh, yes, electronic computers. You can imagine the number of gaps in *those* records. So the only answer I can give to your question, Navigator, is ninety-nine-point-nine-six percent probability of extreme bad luck."

Pilot was seething. "Bad luck? They land here—they drown—and you call it bad luck?"

Coolly, Thinker asked, "Do you think it would be correct to call it *good* luck?"

No sooner had Pilot set the spaceship down on the water than he turned in his chair and faced Thinker. "You really did it this time, Thinker," he sputtered. "You picked the worst planet in the universe! We're out in the middle of nowhere. No people. No trading. What were you thinking?"

Thinker wasn't giving an inch. "I was merely following your orders, Pilot. Perhaps you can think of a plan that will solve your trading problem."

"It's your trading problem, too!" Pilot answered hotly.

"It is my destiny to solve the most difficult problems in all of mathematical science," Thinker replied. "I am not programmed to consider mere trading questions."

For a little while, Thinker was silent, Pilot stewed, and Navigator wondered about things.

Finally, Navigator said, "Thinker? Is there any way we can get any good out of this planet?"

Thinker replied, "Since it's you asking, Navigator, I just may make an exception. Not a complete solution to a trading problem, you understand, that would be beneath me. But for you, a hint. Try this . . . good fortune is sometimes found underfoot."

"Thank you, Thinker," Navigator said. Then he struggled for ten minutes to make sense of the hint, but got nowhere.

Pilot stood up suddenly. Muttering, "Underfoot . . . underfoot," he began to examine the floor of the control room. Every tiny crack, every speck of dust. He found nothing on the floor.

"Underfoot. How far under is underfoot?" Pilot was talking out loud to himself.

The little square shape he found in the rear of the control room was almost invisible. At first, he thought the lines had been drawn on the floor with a ballpoint. But when he ran his fingertip over one of the lines, he felt something. He pulled out his pocketknife and pushed a blade tip into the line. Something moved. The square shape was a trapdoor.

After a struggle, Pilot got the door loose, lifted it, and lowered himself into the dimly lit space below. Nothing but wires and pipes and metal girders. Nothing underfoot but the metal skin of the spaceship. That was the end, except for. . . .

"Yes!" Navigator and Thinker heard him exclaim.

Pilot was silent as he climbed out of the trapdoor, closed it, and walked over to his brother. "Think you can get a straight answer out of Thinker?" he asked softly.

"Oh, sure," Navigator said confidently. "Thinker's always straight with me."

"Ask him if he knows any planets that would pay good money for water," Pilot said.

"Why would anybody do *that*? I mean, water's free . . . Oh, all right, I'll ask."

"A good question," Thinker told Navigator. "Let me review some planetary data. Hmmm. Dam burst, severe shortage of drinking water. No, they'll have that fixed by now. Unexpected drought, need water for irrigation. No, they need too much for a spaceship to help. Oh! Here's one! In fact, I see half a dozen! Planets with three suns! Every fourth or fifth year is dry! No rain, so they store water—but it's very difficult to store *enough*. This one looks good, they're in the middle of a dry year right now."

Thinker told Navigator, "I have one planet where the probability of getting a good price for fresh water at this time is quite high."

Navigator was ecstatic. "Hear that, Pilot? Problem solved! Thinker found a planet where they'll pay for this water!"

"They will *probably* pay," said Thinker modestly. "It's a hundred percent certain that the planet is dry, but only ninety-five-point-three percent certain that they will pay a good price."

"Why would they not pay?" Pilot asked.

"There's a slim chance that another spaceship carrying water could beat us to it," Thinker replied.

"*Probably* is good enough," said Pilot. "With any luck, we can swap a shipload of water for a shipload of trade goods! Or a pile of money! I hate to say it, but—nice going, Thinker!"

"Prepare to fill the main tank and all lateral tanks," he said in a calm voice.

It took all day to fill every tank in the ship.

Then, with the engine struggling bravely to hoist the extra weight, the Famous Space Brothers Original Trading Post took off for a planet so dry it would probably be eager to buy forty million gallons of nice, fresh water.

CHAPTER 16

Long Time No Rain

Partway through the spaceship's flight over Dry Spell—the name the brothers gave the brown, baked planet—they saw a city, high on a hill.

It was, they guessed, about the size of Pittsburgh, where they had once gone with Grandpa. They could see winding riverbeds like Pittsburgh's, and some empty hollows that looked as if they might have been lakes, but they were all bone dry.

Maybe the biggest difference was that Dry Spell was so extremely *sunny*. There is never more than one sun in the sky over Pittsburgh; there were *three* suns close together in the sky over Dry Spell City.

Roads ran from the city in all directions, like the

legs of a spider, but the twins didn't see any cars. A couple of miles down one of the roads was a cluster of long, flat strips of brown earth, large enough for a spaceship.

"There's a place to land," Pilot said.

"I don't see any other spaceships," Navigator pointed out.

"Perfect!" said Pilot. "We'll have the place to ourselves! No competition!"

"What if this isn't where spaceships are supposed to land?" Navigator worried.

"So we'll move," Pilot said nonchalantly. "I think we'll take the spot by that little house. Maybe it's the office. Okay. Ready? Set? GO!"

Five minutes later the ship was on the ground, the dust had settled, and the twins were opening the main entrance doors of the spaceship. A man stepped out of the little house. The sign over the door said CUSTOMS OFFICE.

The man looked a lot like an Earth person, except for his pointy ears—large points at the top and small points at the bottom. Also, there was something different about his skin—it might have been a little bit scaly, like a lizard's skin. But it was hard to be sure about that. Like everything else on Dry Spell, his skin was covered by a layer of brownish dust.

At the foot of the spaceship stairway, the man looked up, saw the twins standing in the main entrance doorway, and called, "Hello, the ship!"

After the usual few exchanges that allowed the twins' brains to figure out the language, the man said, "I'm the customs officer, here to check you in. Permission to come aboard?"

"Come on up," said Navigator, and the customs officer climbed the long flight of stairs.

On the main deck, the first thing he noticed was that he was looking at a couple of kids. So right away he said, "I'll need to speak to your captain."

"I'm the pilot, this is the navigator. We're the owners," Pilot replied shortly. Then, to get the next question over with, he said, "We're thirteen years old."

"Hmmm," said the customs officer. "This the first time you traded here?"

"This is only the third planet we've been on," Navigator answered. "We've done a lot of trading back home, but we're just getting started in space."

"I'm afraid this is not your lucky day, boys," the customs officer said. "It's a bad season for space traders. That's why you don't see any other ships here. It's the same every dry year—everything is slow. The usual cargo—you know, farm machinery, furniture, television games—brings only thirty, forty units."

"What's a unit?" Navigator asked.

"I'm afraid you have a lot to learn," the customs officer said. "Well, I can help you on this. Standard

Trading Units—they're used by all space traders. A unit's a sealed container with two little bars in it. One gold, one platinum. Here, I can show you."

He pulled a small plastic box from his pocket and handed it to Navigator. It was heavy.

"Mind if I take this over there for a minute?" Navigator said, pointing to Thinker. "Just to get an idea of what it's worth."

"No problem," said the customs officer. "While you're doing that, I need your cargo list."

"This isn't all of it," said Pilot as he handed the original cargo list to the customs officer. "This is just what we took when we started out from our home planet."

"What's the rest?" the customs officer asked.

"Just forty million gallons of sweet, fresh drinking water!" said Pilot proudly.

The customs officer grunted as if he had been hit in the stomach. "Oh, boy," he said, taking a little radio from his belt. "We haven't seen that much water all year. The traders in town will go out of their minds. Better get ready for some high-pressure dealing. As soon as they get the word from me, they'll be racing each other to get here."

While the customs officer was talking on his radio, Pilot walked over to where Navigator and Thinker were huddled over the small plastic box.

"We need to know what it's worth in Earth money," Navigator was saying.

Thinker wrapped one of his arms around the box and held it for a few seconds. Then he mentioned a dollar amount that made the twins' eyes pop.

"This is going to be great!" Pilot exclaimed.

"I hope," said Navigator.

"What do you mean?" Pilot asked. "How can we miss?"

"I don't know how this trading's going to work out," Navigator said. "It may not be like the trading we used to do in the store."

"Forget that," Pilot told his brother. "We'll wheel and deal like we always did. You know—all that stuff Grandpa taught us. 'Don't get fancy, stick to the truth. Soften up the other party. He thinks he's your enemy, so make him your friend.' You know it by heart."

"I know, I know," said Navigator. "But I can't help wondering if these traders are going to be tougher."

Pilot laughed. "More high-pressure than we used to get from those traveling salesmen? Rougher than those old farmers we used to buy corn from? No way!"

"Maybe," said Navigator. "We'll see, I guess."

It couldn't have been more than a minute later when the brothers heard the distant sound of big engines starting. Tank trucks by the dozen were pulling out on the road that led to the ship—and, like angry elephants, actually racing each other.

The first trader to reach the ship pointed over his shoulder at his tanks and said, "Twenty thousand gallons. Is this water of yours any good?"

All their trading experience at Grandpa's store had taught the boys not to give a quick answer. Instead, Pilot drew a pitcher of water from the COLD faucet on the hull and handed it to the trucker. He sipped. Then gulped. Then gulped again and again till the pitcher was empty.

While the trader was sampling the water, Pilot told Navigator, "You take this one. I'll be the backup." Then he climbed the stairs into the main entrance of the spaceship.

"How much?" the trader asked.

"Do you prefer warm water or cold?" Navigator asked.

"What's the difference?" the trader asked.

"Well, naturally, warm is higher priced," Navigator replied.

"I can take cold," said the trader.

"Good, then you'll get our lowest price," Navigator said, sounding pleased. "Did you say twenty thousand gallons?"

"Uh-huh," the trader nodded.

"Oh, then you'll get the full quantity discount, too! This is your day for a good deal!" Navigator sounded even more pleased.

The trader liked the sound of that, so he opened the bargaining: "How much are you asking?"

"What's the going rate on this planet right now?" Navigator replied.

"Last time I heard a price, one of our traders got twenty thousand gallons for fourteen units," said the trucker.

"Sounds reasonable—but not this late in the dry season," Navigator said. "That would have been earlier, wouldn't it? When people had their reserve tanks full?"

He had guessed right. The trader tried not to look embarrassed at being caught. "You know, you may be right. Truth is, I don't remember exactly when that was," he said, not looking Navigator in the eye. "I guess the price might be a little higher on this warm a day. How about—oh, maybe I could go as high as twenty-four. Minus that discount."

This was enough to give Navigator, an experienced bargainer, a feel for what the market might possibly pay. He shook his head sadly. "Around fifty-six is the best I can do," he said. "Sounds to me like we're going to have to try some-place else. I saw another big city before we landed here. Well, first I'll try one more trader. Do you mind moving your truck out of the way?"

Both of them knew that the *hard* bargaining was starting.

"I'd hate to go back with an empty tank," said the trader. "My boss would kill me if I paid near that much. I'd probably get fired if I went over thirty."

"Well . . . I shouldn't do this," Navigator said. "But you *were* first in line. I suppose I might let your water go for forty-eight."

The trader appeared to be thinking. "You boys are—how old? Thirteen? Just getting started? That's tough. I'd really like to help you out." He paused and thought some more. "Heck with the boss. I'll make it right with him somehow. Suppose I say thirty-six."

"I don't know," Navigator said, shaking his head. "That's awful low. Let me see if I can get my brother to okay that. He's half owner. I'll do my best, but he's tough."

Navigator climbed the stairs to where Pilot was waiting. "Nice going, Bro," Pilot said.

"He'll go higher," Navigator said, and went back down the stairs, looking sad.

"I'm sorry, I really tried," Navigator said. "But he won't budge. He keeps saying 'Forty-six, forty-six.'"

"Oh, boy," the trader sighed. "I hate to strike out like this. . . . Say! How's this for an idea? You started at fifty-six, I started at twenty-six. What say we split the difference? I'll just tell my boss it was forty-one or nothing, you do the same with your brother."

"You've been real nice," said Navigator. "If you'll forget the discount, I'll fix it with my brother. Straight forty-one, then, okay?"

The trader nodded. Navigator beckoned Pilot down the stairs, and the twins began uncoiling the big hose to fill the truck. It was a normal meeting between two experienced traders. Both felt they had gotten a good deal.

All afternoon, the twins bargained and pumped water, bargained and pumped water. As the suns were getting low, a very long, shiny tank truck pulled up. The sign on the door said BIG AL'S PET FISH SERVICE.

The customs officer had become friendly with the twins, and now he whispered a question: "Do you have criminals on your planet? I mean, big-time?"

"Sure," Pilot said. "Some small-time, some big."

"Well, this is a very big one," the customs officer said in a whisper. "The biggest. He's famous for his pets. Loves them, hates everybody else. He gets mad fast. Be nice to him or he's trouble." He walked out of sight behind the spaceship, looking at the ground so Big Al couldn't get a good look at his face.

The man who got out of the truck wasn't big; he was enormous. He looked like a disgruntled bulldozer as he walked over to the spaceship. He didn't say a word, only scowled darkly at the twins. Pilot hastened to draw a fresh pitcher of water for him.

After tasting the water, Big Al's disposition improved. He nodded, stopped scowling, and said, "I'm having trouble keeping my personal pets healthy. This ought to do it. How much?"

Pilot said, "You want water to keep your pets alive? Terrific! Everybody's been talking about filling swimming pools—all they think about is themselves. But keeping pets alive—that's a really good cause!"

Big Al almost smiled. "You boys ever keep pet fish?"

"Sure did," Pilot replied. "Back on our home planet."

Navigator didn't want Big Al asking about their pet fish—two goldfish that died. So he quickly said, "Hospitals get a ten percent discount, but I like to give pet-fish lovers a little more. Why don't we give you fifteen percent off the regular price?"

Pilot broke in. "Twenty percent. I think we can go twenty percent for this man."

"You're doing the right thing," Big Al said. He almost looked pleased. "It's nice to see young fellows give respect."

"What kinds of pets do you raise?" Navigator asked.

"Sharks and alligators," Big Al replied. "I love sharks and alligators. They're my favorites."

Pilot didn't want to upset Big Al by mentioning that alligators weren't fish, so he tried a subject he was sure Big Al would find interesting. "We never had any pets as big as sharks and alligators. Are they hard to raise?"

Big Al talked a long time about his beloved sharks and alligators. The brothers kept feeding him questions, and Big Al became friendlier as he went along. He finished by saying, "It's nice to see young fellows take an interest in important stuff like sharks and alligators."

"I had no idea they were such good pets," Navigator said.

"They're the best," said Big Al. "People always give respect when they see my sharks and alligators."

Just before he paid the boys and started back, Big Al said, "Don't worry, boys. Being as you were so friendly-like, you can come back anytime. Nobody on this planet will give you trouble."

"Thanks, Big Al," the twins said.

"Mention my name if they try," said Big Al.

"Count on it, Big Al," the twins chorused.

In less than a week, the spaceship had empty water tanks, and a heap—not a mere pile, but a heap—of Standard Trading Units.

"I guess this shows we can make it, all right," Navigator said with a smile.

"Make what?" said Pilot.

"Make it in space! Those were professional traders, and we did okay! We ran into a guy who could have been big trouble, and he only wanted to do favors for us! I think we're going to be a success as space traders!" said Navigator.

"I always knew that," said Pilot. "We're not just going to make it—we're going to be famous! Come on, let's pick the next planet and go! You ready?"

"Not quite," Navigator said. "There's one thing we ought to take care of before we do any more trading."

"Now what?" Pilot said.

"That tax stuff," Navigator explained. "Until we get that straightened out, we're wanted by the law. I hate that feeling."

"How do you think you're going to get it fixed?" Pilot demanded.

"We'll talk to Grandpa," said Navigator.

"He's at the South Pole!" Pilot objected,

"We have the vehicle to get there, don't we?" Navigator replied. "Grandpa will know what to do."

"You hope," Pilot grumbled. But he started getting ready for the fourteen-minute trip back to Earth.

CHAPTER 17

Thinker and the Scientists

When they reached the Antarctic, Pilot didn't like the scenery. "Are you sure you've got us at the right place? We'll never find them in this."

"This" was a few million square miles of Antarctic snow, with only an occasional mountain-top poking out to remind you that there was a whole continent hiding beneath the endless miles of nothing but white.

"They're probably the only expedition in a thousand miles. They ought to stand out." Navigator tried to sound confident.

"I can't see a thing but snow," Pilot said. "This is hopeless. We'll never find them."

Thinker had been standing nearby, watching Pilot and making little clicks of boredom. Now it made a different sound—exasperation—and said, "I have to do everything around here."

"What?" Pilot said sharply. "What's this big thing you have to do?"

"I think," Thinker replied. "I've told you many times to try it, Pilot. Thinking works wonders."

"Oh, yeah?" Pilot snapped angrily. "Does it show you where Grandpa's expedition is?"

"No, it merely tells me where to look," Thinker said. "Look for cliffs."

"Why cliffs?" Pilot wanted to know.

"Fossils are found in rock," said Thinker. "Cliffs are about the only rock that isn't covered with snow."

"Brilliant. Look for cliffs," Pilot said. "That's thinking, huh?"

But a few minutes later, he exclaimed, "Ha! When you're looking for a needle in a haystack, just ask old Eagle Eye! There they are—right at the bottom of that cliff! You can see the tops of their huts!"

"Of course," said Thinker.

"It takes a good eye," said Pilot. Spiraling down, he said, "We're getting a little of everything, Nav. We landed on water, we landed in a desert, now snow. Cool."

"What kind of snow are we landing on?" Navigator asked.

"Snow is snow," Pilot replied confidently.

The spaceship gently kissed the snow. Then gently sank a few feet. Then gently sank a few yards. Then gently sank the rest of the way to the solid ice beneath the great drift of powder snow. The bottom two-thirds of the spaceship was buried.

"Snow is snow, huh?" said Navigator.

"You want a soft landing, you land on soft snow," said Pilot. "No problem."

"I see one," Navigator said. "The snow is blocking the door."

Pilot shrugged. "Big deal, we get a little exercise. Come on, let's get the shovels."

It took the brothers thirty minutes of digging to make a tunnel—it slanted upwards—from the spaceship entrance to daylight. "I wonder what Grandpa will say when he sees us," Navigator said, panting.

"Same as when we got lost at the big arts festival in Pittsburgh," Pilot said. "You remember. He starts off angry, then he's real happy that we're okay, then he wants to know all about everything we saw."

Along with the other expedition scientists, Grandpa was waiting when the twins broke out into the cold sunshine.

He looked astonished. To the scientist next to him, he exclaimed, "I told you! It was true! All that insane stuff on the Internet wasn't a fake!"

To the boys, his first words were loud and angry, "You two are in trouble! That crazy takeoff?

Flying a spaceship? You don't even have a driver's license! What were you *thinking?*"

Then, hugging his grandsons until they turned red, he said, "I'm so glad to see you safe, I can't tell you! Anybody hurt? Are you okay?"

Then, without a pause, "Quite a spaceship you've got here. How fast will it go? What kind of mileage do you get? What's it like inside?"

"Did I call it or did I call it?" Pilot murmured to his brother.

"It really was an emergency, Grandpa," Navigator said.

"I know," said Grandpa. "Mr. Prefer, the TV guy, told me what really happened. He just finished interviewing me—by email, can you imagine? He thinks you boys are the best thing that ever happened. That spaceship story made him famous. He doesn't like the tax collector at all."

"We still have a problem back in Pennsylvania, Grandpa," Navigator said.

"I know. Maybe we can figure something out," Grandpa said. "Right now, let's see this spaceship of yours."

Going through the spaceship, the scientists were loud and hilarious. To them, it was a scientific amusement park. They tried every gadget on the ship. They shouted when they saw the metal paper smooth itself out after it was crumpled. The Polish scientist and the Nigerian scientist each took a turn on the language machine, then tested it scientifically—by learning to speak each other's languages. Roars of laughter all around.

But the biggest hit with the scientists was the tall robot. They flocked around Thinker and treated it like the smartest professor who ever lived. They asked countless scientific questions. Thinker answered with an air of wisdom. When the scientists nodded reverently, Thinker's screen glowed briefly with the little pink beam of pleasure that only flattery could produce.

One scientist asked Thinker how planet Earth compared to other planets. "I don't know too much about your planet," Thinker replied. "Let me see . . . what's the main way people travel?"

"Cars and planes," the scientist answered.

"Cars with wheels? Planes with wings?"

"That's correct," the scientist replied.

"No levity carriers at all?" Thinker sounded surprised.

Pilot interrupted. "What's levity?"

"The opposite of gravity," Thinker said coolly. "Never mind that, Pilot, these scientists might understand levity, but you're not ready for it."

Turning to the scientist who had asked about Earth, Thinker said, "I believe your planet would be classified as a semi-primitive, grade seven."

The chief was silent while Grandpa described the boys' tax problem back in Pennsylvania. He stayed silent while the scientists offered one idea after another. Each was discarded. When the chief finally spoke, he rumbled, "I know the governor of Pennsylvania."

Everybody stopped and listened. The chief had that effect on people.

"The governor wanted to start a Pennsylvania Dinosaur Museum," the chief continued. "He didn't care about dinosaurs, just about the jobs a museum could bring. He'd give anything for more jobs in Pennsylvania."

"What's the governor like?" Grandpa asked.

"Somehow, he reminds me of a man I knew long ago," said the chief. "He was an old horse-trader who used to come around when I was a boy on the farm. He loved making deals. That was the most fun he got out of life. If he only traded a dog for a duck, he was happy."

Grandpa looked puzzled. The chief rolled on. "He was a tough bargainer. And clever. But I remember a couple of times when my father decided in advance that he would pretend he didn't really care to trade. He walked away, and the old horse-trader followed him. Dad didn't get taken those times. He may even have come out ahead."

The boys could tell that Grandpa was thinking hard. "I suppose we could use that approach on the governor—play hard to get. But we'd have to have something he wanted."

Thinker whispered to Navigator, "Remind them about the metal paper."

Navigator crumpled the sheet and tossed it on the table. It smoothed out with a little snap. "This doesn't go with the ship. It belongs to us."

Grandpa picked it up. "This is great stuff, but it's only one sheet. If we knew how to make it by the ton, then we'd have something to deal with. But without that, I don't think. . . ."

"I know how," Thinker said quietly. Everybody stared at the robot. "Just one of the useful little tricks I keep in my memory."

"It's an interesting special paper, Thinker," Grandpa said, "It looks very expensive. But. . . ."

"It isn't expensive to make," Thinker replied. "And it can be more than paper. You can make it as thick as you want."

"I'm not sure what good that would do us. I mean—to impress the governor, we'd need something that meant lots of jobs."

"Well," Thinker said, "those wheeled cars you use to get around? Do they ever get scratched and dented?"

A little chuckle ran around the table. "They sure do," Grandpa replied. "Happens all the time."

Thinker continued. "What if the scratches and

dents smoothed out and disappeared, all by themselves? Would that impress the governor?"

There was silence around the table while the scientists thought about a world in which cars got banged and scraped as often as they do now—but the damage disappeared in seconds.

"If it's really that good, it's going to take big factories to make it," Grandpa said. "Lots of jobs."

"Betcha the governor would trade a bundle for that," said Pilot.

"If we can get through on the satellite phone," said the Chief, "I think I could arrange a meeting for you with the governor. You'd need to plan your presentation carefully," he added.

"I think we'd better rehearse," said Grandpa.

The meeting took place in the governor's office.

Alton J. Weberschreber sat behind the governor. He looked just as solemn as he had when the twins first met him, but angrier. He was there, the governor explained, to advise him about sales tax rules and regulations.

Pilot and Navigator sat in front of the governor's desk. Grandpa sat behind them. The twins had expected him to do the talking, but he surprised them. "Not a chance, boys. If you're going to be space traders, you'll be dealing with a lot of tough customers like the governor. I'll help if I have to. But this is your job."

The governor spoke first and tried to end the meeting before it started. "I know all about the spaceship and the tax situation, boys. I'm sorry and all that, but the state needs the money. And the law is the law. We have to collect taxes. And that means we have to take the ship. Anything else you want to talk about?"

"We came to make a deal," Pilot said with the same firm expression he had rehearsed. "A trade. We give you something Pennsylvania needs, and that covers the tax."

Alton J. Weberschreber snickered. He could make even a snicker sound dull. "What can you trade when we own the ship?"

"The secret of making this stuff," Pilot said, crumpling the metal paper and tossing it on the governor's desk. "This doesn't go with the ship. It belongs to us."

"What is it?" the governor asked, crumpling the sheet and watching it smooth out.

"Think of it as a new material for car bodies," Navigator said. He had memorized this part for the meeting. "Hoods and fenders and doors that repair their own dents and scratches."

The governor looked interested.

Navigator continued. "All made in Pennsylvania factories—because Pennsylvania owns the patent."

The governor sat up straight.

Just as they had rehearsed, Grandpa held up a sheet of paper. "These are the instructions for making it. It's quite simple. The first year, maybe you'd only make—oh, front fenders. Say ten million cars are produced in a year—twenty million front fenders. How many Pennsylvania jobs do you suppose that would come to, governor?"

The governor's eyes gleamed, but the boys could see that he wasn't ready to bite. "It sounds risky. Suppose this wonder material doesn't work out?"

"Besides," Alton J. Weberschreber said, "you still owe one million, eight hundred thousand, nine hundred and sixty dollars. And twenty-nine cents. With interest that would come to . . . " He started to press buttons on a little calculator.

"Never mind that, it doesn't matter," Grandpa said, with a nod to Pilot.

The nod was Pilot's cue. Just as rehearsed, he took the metal paper from the governor's hands and stood up to go. "Well, thanks anyway, governor, but if we can't agree on the spaceship, we'll have to see if we can make a deal with someone else." He paused. "Maybe some other state."

"We thought we ought to give Pennsylvania the first chance," Grandpa said. "Let's go, boys."

Those words were another cue they had

rehearsed. All together, Pilot, Navigator, and Grandpa stood up. "I have reason to believe that Ohio is interested," Grandpa said.

"Hold on, fellows," the governor said quickly. "Let's not be hasty. Give us a minute here."

He leaned toward Alton J. Weberschreber. They began an intense whispered conversation. The governor's face went from red to white to purple and back to red. Alton's face went from angry to scared to thoughtful to delighted. Finally they shook hands, and Alton J. Weberschreber started scribbling rapidly.

The governor looked at Grandpa, and said, "One other small matter, sir. That sheet mentions a Pennsylvania Spaceship Museum. I believe the location is your farm. Would you be willing to leave that land to the state for a museum, if it means saving the deal for these boys?"

Grandpa looked at the twins. They looked back, hoping a message was visible in their eyes: Don't worry about the farm, the spaceship is all we need.

Grandpa laughed. "The chief was right, governor. You're a hard bargainer. Sure, I'll do that."

The governor beamed. "Then you've got a deal, boys. In fact, we've all got a deal." He put his hand on Alton's shoulder. "I'd like you-all to meet my friend Alton J. Weberschreber, the new head tax collector for the North-central District. He has come up with a nice, neat way to make this work legally.

He's writing up the agreement, and we'll all sign it as soon as you turn over this secret. You give us a little time to make some test fenders. If this stuff works, the tax will be wiped out, and the ship will be all yours."

The governor smiled the smile that had gotten him one-point-three million more votes than the other guy in the last election and asked, "Is everybody happy?"

Everybody was.

CHAPTER 19

Dead or Alive—
Choose One

The spaceship was parked right where the twins first saw it, behind Grandpa's old farmhouse. They were sitting in the control room with Grandpa.

"Come on, Grandpa," Navigator coaxed. "You still have six days' leave from the Antarctic. Plenty of time to cruise around a few planets."

It was Pilot's turn to coax, "We could take a little spin, then drop you off right by your expedition. On time."

"It would take longer than that to get from here to Mars," Grandpa objected. "And I don't think that I'd be interested in Mars."

The boys explained about getting to any distant galaxy in fourteen minutes.

"What kind of planet would interest you?" Thinker asked. It liked Grandpa.

"Thanks for asking, Thinker, but probably none. Unless . . . are there any planets that still have dinosaurs?"

"Dozens," Thinker said. "And that's just the ones that aren't mostly covered by glaciers or erupting volcanoes."

"How big?" asked Grandpa. "The dinosaurs, I mean."

"Let me explain it this way," said Thinker. "If *Tyrannosaurus Rex* was size medium, these would be extra large."

"Well. . . ." Grandpa was hooked. He could see himself bringing back a history-making discovery.

"You really should consider one more question before we start," Thinker said.

There was silence. Everybody waited for the question.

"Alive or dead?" Thinker asked.

"You mean—" Everybody waited to hear what Thinker meant.

"That's right," Thinker explained. "Do you want to visit live dinosaurs or fossils?"

"Live, of course!" Pilot shouted.

"Fossils, we'll take fossils," Navigator said quickly.

Grandpa wanted to know more before he decided. "Those really big dinosaurs—are they meat-eaters?"

"Oh my, yes," Thinker replied. "They gobble meat."

"Do they move very fast?" Grandpa asked.

"About six miles an hour tops, if you call that fast," Thinker said.

"Not really," Grandpa said. "It shouldn't be too hard to avoid them. . . . Is it?"

"They have a move like that ridiculous game Pilot likes. Football, isn't that what it's called?" said Thinker.

"Football isn't ridiculous!" Pilot said.

Thinker ignored Pilot. "Any time one of these giant dinosaurs gets fairly close to its prey, it moves like a slow lineman trying to tackle a fast quarterback—he tries to fall on him."

"The quarterback usually gets away," said Grandpa.

"Not when the lineman weighs eighty tons," said Thinker.

Grandpa nodded decisively. "That settles it. Boys, let's go see a planet where we can find some nice fossils."

Grandpa's face took on a faraway look. "You know, I've never been able to top the chief. I'd find a nice fossil; he'd find a better one. I'd like to bring back the skull of a fossil dinosaur big enough to eat his *Tyrannosaurus Rex* for breakfast."

So they went.

And he did.

Almost the End

CHAPTER 20

An Extra Credit Puzzle

Readers of this story may have noticed a mysterious fact. Anyway, it looks like a fact, and it raises a puzzling question:

How could the Space Brothers get a spaceship after J. and V. Smith made it famous, but before Junior and Vernon Smith ever began making it famous?

Sadly, not even the most far-out scientists and mathematicians have ever figured out the answer.

(Thinker knows but is programmed not to tell.)

If you should happen to come up with the solution, kindly send it to the person most likely to be curious about it:

Chief Curator
Classic Spaceship Museum
Whipple Crossing
Pennsylvania, USA.

Be sure to print on the envelope, in large block letters—

POSTMASTER, PLEASE HOLD
TO BE MAILED IN JANUARY, 3005.

Don't forget the stamp. The post office will not deliver mail without postage.

(How much postage? No problem. If you are clever enough to solve this puzzle, you will surely be able to figure out how many stamps to put on the envelope.)

The Very End